P9-DMZ-711

ALSO BY POLLY HORVATH

The Canning Season

Everything on a Waffle

The Trolls

When the Circus Came to Town

The Happy Yellow Car

No More Cornflakes

An Occasional Cow
with pictures by Gioia Fiammenghi

The Vacation

The Corps of the Bare-Boned Plane

The Pepins and Their Problems

the PePiNS AND their PROBLEMS

by POLLY HORVATH

pictures by
MARYLIN HAFNER

Farrar, Straus and Giroux

SQUARE
FISH

Portions of this work originally appeared, in somewhat
different form, in *Cricket* magazine.

ᴴᴾ
SQUARE
FISH

An Imprint of Macmillan

Originally published in the United States by Farrar, Straus and Giroux
First Square Fish Edition: March 2008
Designed by Barbara Grzeslo
Square Fish logo designed by Filomena Tuosto
10 9 8 7 6 5 4 3 2 1
www.squarefishbooks.com

Library of Congress Cataloging-in-Publication Data
Horvath, Polly.
    The Pepins and their problems / Polly Horvath ; pictures by
Marylin Hafner.— 1st ed.
        p.   cm.
    "Portions of this work . . . originally appeared in Cricket
magazine"—T.p. verso.
    Summary: The unusual Pepin family confront numerous
problems, such as having a cow who creates lemonade rather
than milk and having to cope with a competitive neighbor, and
the reader is invited to help them solve them.
    ISBN-13: 978-0-312-37751-9
    ISBN-10: 0-312-37751-7
    [1. Problem solving—Fiction.   2. Neighbors—Fiction.
3. Humorous stories.]   I. Hafner, Marylin, ill.   II. Title.

PZ7.H79224Pe 2004
[Fic]—dc22
                                                   2003060196

To Margaret Ferguson

Contents

The Pepins and Their Problems

TOADS in their SHOES

There are always problems in the lives of Mr. and Mrs. Pepin; their children, Petunia and Irving; their dog, Roy; their cat, Miranda; and their very fine neighbor Mr. Bradshaw. Now, all families have problems, and all families, one hopes, eventually solve them, but the Pepins and their very fine neighbor Mr. Bradshaw have problems of such a bizarre nature that they are never able to find a solution and get on with their lives without the help of you, dear reader.

Just recently the Pepins awoke to find toads in their shoes. This was quite a puzzler.

"What shall we do?" asked Mrs. Pepin, who needed to put her shoes on so she could catch the 8:05 train to her part-time job at the Domestic Laboratory, on the outskirts of beautiful downtown Peony, where she led the field in peanut butter experiments. The Domestic Laboratory was not a strict company, but it did require its workers to arrive shod.

"What shall we do?" asked Mr. Pepin, who needed his shoes so he could drive them both to the train station. There he would catch the 8:10 to work at the cardboard factory, where he was in charge of corrugation.

"I am not putting my foot in a toad-filled shoe," said Petunia, who was in the fifth grade, where she wasn't in charge of anything.

"Maybe we should go next door and ask Mr. Bradshaw if he has toads in his shoes," said

Irving, who was a sixth-grade genius and in charge of leading all charges.

In the end, that is what the Pepins did. They went next door to their very fine neighbor Mr. Bradshaw, who was eating corn twinklies and hadn't looked at his shoes yet. The Pepins explained to Mr. Bradshaw what the problem was, and together they went to examine Mr. Bradshaw's very fine shoes. There were toads in every single pair. Even in the galoshes.

"Thank you for calling this to my attention," said Mr. Bradshaw, and then, because he was an exemplary host as well as a very fine neighbor, he poured bowls of corn twinklies all round.

The Pepins and Mr. Bradshaw could not imagine what to do with their toad-filled shoes. How had the toads gotten into all the shoes, and how were the Pepins to get them out? They thought for a very long while, but even Irving the genius was unable to think of a solution.

This is where I must ask for your assistance, dear reader. Many, many books are written to be read passively. The author discourages reader input. The author actively dislikes it. Shoo, shoo, says

the author to his pesky readers. But then most books, one could almost say all others, are not written about the Pepins, and therefore the characters do not need help. Or if they need it, the characters seem to think they must persevere on their own with silent dignity. Not so the Pepins. The Pepins love help in solving their problems, by which they mean having others aid them in their endless speculations. Could this be? Could that be? How does one get down off a duck? Or get toads out of one's shoes?

Fortunately, this author is endowed with unusually large psychic antennae. She is deeply attuned to her readers. If you put one finger on each temple and concentrate, she will be able to hear your solution and share it with the Pepins and other readers. No other author on the face of the earth is able to do this. Do not expect it of them.

So go ahead, think your solutions very hard, think them northward because your author lives, most likely, above you. No, not in heaven, angelic though she is, but in Canada. Although to hear some Canadians, you'd think the two were interchangeable. Just do not get carried away and shout them out loud if your parents are asleep, because it is past your bedtime and you are reading this book under your covers by flashlight. I, your author, do not wish to get in trouble.

Wait! I hear readers!

As usual, explanations come more easily than solutions. Our readers are rife with explanations, but I do not hear any solutions per se. That is fine. I welcome all input: solutions, explanations, answers, questions, speculations. A writer's life is a lonely one.

A reader from Tinton Falls, New Jersey, thinks an ecological problem has caused a sudden growth in the toad population, although a reader from Lake Nebagamon, Wisconsin, asks why the toads have taken to shoes.

A reader from Normal, Illinois, thinks Irving has secretly filled the shoes with toads. I'm afraid this idea must be disregarded, as Irving, apart from being a genius, is a model citizen. But we can certainly see what kinds of tricks some of our readers would be up to if not carefully watched.

A reader from Wiggonsville, Ohio, thinks that

aliens from space had put tadpoles in the shoes, and the toads had *grown* there. I'm afraid that readers from Pottsville, Pennsylvania; Vinton, Iowa; Miami, Oklahoma (please stop shouting that Miami is in Florida. There is *too* a Miami, Oklahoma. If you don't believe me, get out your atlas)—anyway, I'm afraid that all these readers also insist that the aliens have been at it, and to them I say, and listen closely because I am only going to say this once, *nobody*, not even an alien, has *that* much time.

The correct answer comes from a dear reader in Kalamazoo, Michigan, who suggests that the toads have merely run out of toadstools to sit on and are hiding in shoes until more toadstools are made ready. Once the Pepins and their very fine neighbor Mr. Bradshaw were apprised of this, they ran (barefoot) to the nearest woods and found toadstools to lure the toads out of their shoes. Everyone was late for work and school, but at least they arrived shod.

A day that begins with toads in the shoes is a long one. The Pepins were tired that evening, and so was their very fine neighbor Mr. Bradshaw. All were ready to retire to bed early when Petunia, who had a keen aesthetic sense (meaning she sometimes saw pretty things even where no pretty things existed), noticed the beginning of a magnificent sunset.

"Mom, Dad, Irving, Miranda, Roy," she called, "this small picture window doesn't do the night sky justice. Let us all climb up on the roof to see the whole horizon. Roy, go next door and fetch Mr. Bradshaw."

Roy went next door immediately. The Pepins, when they were teaching Roy to sit and stay, also taught him the go-next-door-and-fetch-Mr.-Bradshaw command. Mr. Bradshaw came over at once and helped the Pepins put a ladder against the side of the house. Everyone climbed up to the roof. Irving carried Roy, and Petunia carried Miranda. Mr. Pepin carried Mrs. Pepin, even though she did not particularly want to be carried, but just to round things out. Mr. Bradshaw, who had no one to carry, stole a squirrel. Mr. and Mrs. Pepin were the last ones up, and after Mr. Pepin put Mrs. Pepin down, he turned around to look at the sunset and accidentally kicked the ladder, which fell all the way to the ground with a great *clunk*. The Pepins and Mr. Bradshaw were stuck on the roof. Of course, they could think of no way down.

"What a thing to happen," said Mrs. Pepin, "on a day that began with toads in our shoes."

As it became evident that they were not going to get off the roof that night, Mrs. Pepin turned to her very fine neighbor and said, "Dear Mr. Bradshaw, I had always hoped that if we were someday fortunate enough to have you as our houseguest, we would at least be able to serve you a little cheese. Nevertheless, won't you be our roofguest tonight?"

"Dear lady," replied Mr. Bradshaw, "I do not see that I have a choice."

Or does he? Put your fingers to your temples, dear reader, and please help me solve this Pepin problem.

GRiLLED Lemonade SANDWiches, Anyone?

Many readers have thought their solutions in your author's direction. She is positively aswamp and cannot mention them all. But we will go over a few.

A reader from Grow, Texas, thinks the Pepins should build an identical house next to their own but with a fire escape. Then they could leap over to the new roof and climb down the fire escape. Hmmm.

A reader from North Livermore, Maine, suggests the Pepins cover themselves in bear grease and slither through the downspout. Even if the

Pepins could fit into the downspout, they probably would have more difficulty than the residents of North Livermore finding bear grease on their roof. Geography is everything. Oh, and another thing, as far as your author is concerned: if we are going to liver, liver less rather than more.

A reader from Miami, Missouri (YES! I could hardly believe it: there are people wearing white shoes and working on their tans in Missouri, too!), thinks that if the Pepins don't mind taking off all their clothes and tying them together, they can make a rope. The Pepins stop the author right here. They do not want to take off their clothes. Well, of course not. Perhaps, says Mrs. Pepin gently, we should try to find our own solution. And so they do.

Miranda and Roy found some old newspaper in the roof's gutter and constructed a lightweight, motorless aircraft. They sailed off in the sweet twilight air and were later seen in New Jersey.

Irving the genius hit upon bungee jumping—a fad that had swept through Peony like milk through a straw.

"Ah, bungee jumping, my good Irving," said

their very fine neighbor Mr. Bradshaw. "How in-
genious. How do you suggest we go about this
jump of the bunge?"

"It is quite simple," said Irving, screwing up his
forehead in that thoughtful way of his. "First we tie
something cordlike around our waists. Then we
leap headfirst off the roof."

"How very interesting," said Mrs. Pepin, turning to Mr. Pepin. "He always did have a remarkable
IQ."

"Remarkable," said Mr. Pepin. "He was born
with his eyes open."

"Wide open," said Mrs. Pepin.

"What shall we use for cord?" asked Petunia, looking around the bare roof.

There was naught but the belts the gentlemen wore. At a glance, those brainy Pepins could tell the belts were inadequate.

"I have some cord in the garage," said Mr. Pepin.

"It's a pity we can't get it from here," said Mrs. Pepin, gazing down at the crowd that had gathered below to watch.

"I'll fetch it for you!" called Mr. Quinn, another of the Pepins' fine neighbors.

"How did you get stuck up there in the first place?" yelled another man.

"Our ladder fell," said Mrs. Pepin, pointing to the ladder lying useless in the yard.

"Ah," someone said.

"Pity," said another, giving the ladder a kick.

"Could happen to anyone."

"I think it was rather careless of them," came one sour note. "What are they going to do now? We might have to call the Red Cross."

"The question is how to get them down," corrected another uplooker, gently bringing the conversation back on track.

"Or who knows how long they'll be stuck there," someone else agreed. "We must work while we still have the last of daylight's fading glory." Peony was full of poets.

"Those children might miss school tomorrow if it takes too long."

"May never graduate if it *really* takes too long."

Mr. Quinn fetched the rope and cut it into lengths with his pocketknife. He put the ladder back against the house, and while Mayor Reynolds steadied it, he climbed up to deliver the pieces

of rope. Then he climbed down, put the ladder back on the ground, and rejoined the crowd. The Pepins tied the cords around their waists. Mr. Pepin checked that all knots were secure.

"WAIT A SECOND!" yelled someone from the crowd. "THIS WILL NEVER WORK!"

The Pepins and their very fine neighbor Mr. Bradshaw, poised at the edge of the roof preparing to jump, straightened up and called down, "Why not?"

"The ropes should be attached to your *ankles*," called the same voice in the wilderness. "The point of bungee jumping is to land *upside down*."

"Ah," murmured the crowd.

"Ah," murmured the Pepins.

"You don't say," said Mr. Bradshaw.

It was the work of a few moments to reattach the ropes to their ankles, and the Pepins and Mr. Bradshaw stood again poised for flight.

"ONE . . ." shouted the crowd helpfully. "TWO . . ." But before they reached three, there came a cry from a squeaky-voiced girl. It was Viola Squawk, the reddest-haired, most freckle-faced of the Peony Squawks.

"I wouldn't do that if I were you!" she called.

The crowd turned to her. "My dear child, we have it all thought out," said Mr. Pepin in his kindly manner.

The crowd rallied and repeated, "ONE . . . TWO . . ."

"You'll be sorry!" squeaked Squawk.

"Yes, yes, whatever is it now?" said Mr. Pepin testily. He was getting tired of bending over and straightening up.

"There's just one little thing you have forgotten, but it may come in handy," said Viola, who had whipped out a bottle of purple nail polish and was nonchalantly painting her nails.

"To say a prayer?" guessed a crowd member, dropping to his knees.

"To check weather conditions?" said another, licking her finger and holding it up to see which way the wind blew.

"To get a permit from town hall?" asked Mayor Reynolds, trying to remember if there was such a thing.

"*Au contraire, au contraire,*" said Viola, pausing dramatically to blow on her wet nails.

During this dramatic pause, can you, dear reader, think what the bungee jumpers had forgotten in their haste to bunge?

Yes, quite right. They had not tied the other ends of their ropes to anything. Instead of dangling delicately upside down, they would have landed on their heads. It would have mussed their hairdos considerably.

"Ah yes," said Mr. Bradshaw, peering about. "But there doesn't seem to be anything to tie the ropes *to.*"

"I know," said Irving, that great brain of his ever active. "If someone could fetch a pikestaff, we could drive it into the roof and all tie our ropes to it."

"A what?" called someone from the crowd.

"A pikestaff," grumbled another crowd member. "Whoever heard of such a thing in these parts?"

"Sounds like something from medieval days," said the town librarian.

"I happen to have one in my garage," said a fourth party. "Back in a jiff."

The man with the pikestaff returned triumphantly. It's always a good feeling to save the day with odds and ends from one's garage. Mayor Reynolds and Mr. Quinn put the ladder up once more and steadied it while the gentleman delivered his pikestaff. He even helped Irving drive it into the roof before descending again to the ground.

"Thanks very much," said Irving as the Pepins and Mr. Bradshaw tied their ropes to the pikestaff. "Now, if you could just get that ladder out of our way."

"Of course," said the owner of the pikestaff, blushing, and moving it so no one would bang into it on the way down.

The Pepins prepared once more for flight.

"STOP!" yelled Viola, who had taken off her shoes during this interlude and painted all her toenails as well. "Anyone with pikestaff experience can tell you

20

it will not support the weight of five bungee jumpers."

"Oh," said the Pepins and Mr. Bradshaw.

"Ah," said the crowd.

"I have taken the liberty of calling the fire department. They will be here shortly," said Viola.

The fire department arrived. All of the firefighters were as bright as new pennies, and when they were unable to convince the Pepins to leap into a net, they put the ladder back up and coaxed the Pepins down.

"The ladder," said Irving the genius. "Of course!"

It was not a spectacular descent. "But," said Mrs. Pepin as she later related the story to a party of hat-wearing tea drinkers, "we were all a bit tired by then."

• • •

The next Saturday at lunch, Mr. Pepin said, "There is still some unfinished business from the contretemps on the roof."

"Is there indeed?" said Mrs. Pepin.

"We have yet to offer our very fine neighbor Mr. Bradshaw his bit of cheese," said Mr. Pepin.

Petunia gave Roy, recently returned from New Jersey with Miranda, the go-next-door-and-fetch-Mr.-Bradshaw command. Irving leaped up and opened the refrigerator. A search for cheese was fruitless. And cheeseless.

"We are out of cheese," he announced.

"Can it be?" asked Mrs. Pepin. "We must quickly make some more. Mr. Bradshaw will soon be on his way."

The Pepins are a superior family for many reasons, not the least of which is that they make their own cheese. They keep a cow named Nelly in their backyard. Nelly's milk is used exclusively for cheese. The family raced outside and explained the situation to her.

"Normally, of course," Mrs. Pepin said, "we only ask you for milk at daybreak. But Mr. Bradshaw is on his way. We have denied him cheese once. I hate to think what would happen if we denied him again."

"What *do* you think would happen?" asked Mr. Pepin, turning in alarm to Mrs. Pepin.

"With cheese, one never knows," said Mrs. Pepin.

Nelly, who was an understanding cow, allowed Petunia to milk her, even though, as she murmured, it was the time of afternoon she usually liked to watch soap operas. Petunia stood up in alarm.

"Mother, Father, Irving," she gasped, "Nelly has no milk!"

"What is that liquid hitting the bucket, then?" asked Irving, taking a closer look.

"Good golly," said Mr. Pepin, dipping in a finger and tasting it. "It's lemonade!"

"Nelly, at any other time this would be amusing," said Mrs. Pepin. "But right now we need cheese."

"Yes, Nelly," said Petunia, raising an admonishing finger. "Cut this out immediately."

"Goodness, you don't think I did that on purpose, do you?" asked Nelly, stalking away in disgust.

Mrs. Pepin rushed the lemonade over to the cheesemaker. What came out was little squares of solid lemonade, rather like Jell-O. It was nothing you could serve with a good claret. She nibbled one experimentally. "You can cut it into cubes and stick toothpicks in it, but it will fool nobody."

"Whatever are we to do?" cried Petunia, for just then she spied Roy approaching with Mr. Bradshaw.

I don't wish to trouble you, dear reader, but I am on my way to a cotillion and the Pepins have begged me to ask you what you think they should do under such cheeseless circumstances.

THE DAPPER MAN AT THE DOOR

As usual, readers have been busy. But please, please try to concentrate on the Pepins. I am tired of being sent recipes for cheese doodles and gripes about fractions, etc., that have nothing to do with our heroes' problems. I agree with our reader in Walkerton, Indiana, that of all the ways to spend your time, fractions are probably the least productive, so let's just NOT THINK ABOUT THEM and get back to cheese! Perhaps it would help if everyone just closed his or her eyes and removed all extraneous wiggle-waggle from his or her brain. There, now don't you feel better?

A reader from Mendota Heights, Minnesota, thinks the Pepins should forget cheese, which is too high in cholesterol anyway, and just serve a few raisins and odds and ends from the bottom of the bread box. Right, says Mr. Pepin, don't believe I shall be attending any of *his* parties.

A reader from Hughes, Alaska, suggests serving snow. I feel that everyone has lost track of the point. The point, the *point*, dear reader, is to produce cheese. But thank you all very much anyway. Always nice to hear from you.

"What shall we do? What shall we do?" cried Mrs. Pepin as their very fine neighbor Mr. Bradshaw approached the barn.

"You must think quickly, my dear," said Mr. Pepin. "Mr. Bradshaw can now be seen with the naked eye."

"Hurry, hurry," said Petunia, putting down her binoculars.

"I know!" screamed Mrs. Pepin, leaping over the milk stool in her excitement. "Petunia, run to the store and buy some processed cheese cubes. While you are gone, I will entertain our very fine neighbor Mr. Bradshaw with my Portuguese scarf dance."

"Your what?" said Mr. Pepin, who was astounded to find that after fifteen years of marriage his wife could still surprise him with unexpected talents.

"Yes, many years ago my mother insisted that all her children learn to do Portuguese scarf dances. In case of emergency. 'You never know, my little cauliflower ears'—as she affectionately called us—'when you will have an urgent need to entertain.' And how right she was."

So while Petunia ran to the store, Mrs. Pepin gathered all the scarves to be found in the barn. After greeting Mr. Bradshaw and inviting him to sit, she swished and swashed to Mr. Pepin's gentle crooning of "The Battle Hymn of the Republic," which was the song he liked best. Soon they all took up the tune: Mrs. Pepin (proving she could swish, swash, and sing at the same time—an added bonus); Irving, who in his genius-like way added harmony; Roy and Miranda, who were taking hula lessons, throwing in some interesting Hawaiian sign language; and Mr. Bradshaw, who claimed he hadn't had a day in the barn like this for *quite* some time. Even Nelly joined in with an occasional bar. When Petunia returned, somewhat out of breath and harried, the party was in full swing.

"One more time!" cried Mr. Bradshaw. Mrs. Pepin handed him a scarf, imparted a few hasty instructions on when to swish and when to swash, and dashed into the house to arrange a cheese platter.

"Alas," said Petunia, "due to the Peony winetasting festival, there is not a piece of cheese to be had in town."

"Oh, wouldn't you know it," said Mrs. Pepin. "Whatever shall we do?"

"We will simply have to use the lemonade cheese," said Petunia, "and hope Mr. Bradshaw doesn't notice."

"I'll tell you what," said Mrs. Pepin, who was seldom at a loss. "We will put a pear on the platter."

"A pear?" said Petunia.

"A pear to trick the eye," said Mrs. Pepin. "When Mr. Bradshaw sees many cubes with toothpicks in them surrounding a pear, he will say to himself, 'Where there's pear, there must be cheese!' "

"I am dubious," said Petunia. But she searched the refrigerator for a pear.

"Mother, we have no pears," she said at last.

"You must run to the store and buy one," said Mrs. Pepin. She peered out the window. The scarf dancing was still going on at a furious rate. Several other neighbors had joined the throng. Mayor Reynolds and Viola Squawk were circling each other holding opposite ends of a scarf between their teeth. "I will go out and be distracting in my wholesome way. When you return, arrange lemonade squares with toothpicks in them on my best cheese board and put a pear in the middle."

Petunia raced back to town, and Mrs. Pepin returned to the barn, where she made up dances as fast as she could. Several relied rather heavily on the twist.

Finally Mr. Bradshaw sat down with a thump on a bale of hay. "I can go no longer," he said, wiping his dewy brow with the scarf he had been waving about. "How I wish I had a bit of cheese."

This was as broad a hint as a hostess could hope to find. Mrs. Pepin ignored it and said, "Oh, now, Mr. Bradshaw, surely there is a cha-cha-cha still hovering in your soul."

"Not a cha," said Mr. Bradshaw, wearily licking his lips.

Mrs. Pepin glanced nervously out the window. No Petunia in sight.

"Let's go to the hop, oh, baby! Let's go to the hop!" sang Mrs. Pepin, desperately grabbing the hands of those who had fallen prostrate upon farm implements. But no one rose. Only Mrs. Pepin and Nelly danced and sang. The rest politely wondered when the cheese would be served.

Just when Nelly thought her hooves would give out, Petunia burst through the door carrying the cheese board, on which rested many squares of

lemonade cheese and a pear to trick the eye. The neighbors who had impulsively joined the boisterous merrymaking suddenly realized they were uninvited and rose as a group to go. Mrs. Pepin said, "Oh, do stay," but no one thought for a moment that she meant it.

When they had departed, Mr. Bradshaw sighed, took several cubes, and gobbled them right down. The swishing had made him very hungry, and the swashing had left him nearly starving. It wasn't, therefore, until he was on his fourth or fifth cube that he said, "How extraordinary! This is cheese, and yet it is not."

"Look at the pear!" said Mrs. Pepin, bursting into tears.

"But this is delicious! Delightful! Why, I must know where you got it. Bradshaw's Unusual and Extraordinary Snack Products will never be the same."

For, as it turned out, Mr. Bradshaw was the president of his own company, known as Bradshaw's Unusual and Extraordinary Snack Products: makers of the edible lightbulb. Naturally, the Pepins were all familiar with this line of crunch and munch, but never once guessed that its founder and president was their very fine neighbor Mr. Bradshaw.

"This lemonade cheese, for such I divine it is," said Mr. Bradshaw, tasting and analyzing, "will make us a fortune."

The Pepins fell all over one another explaining how Nelly had given lemonade instead of milk and how circumstances had necessitated putting it in the cheesemaker.

"What a wonderful happenstance!" said their very fine neighbor Mr. Bradshaw. "You'll be rich beyond your wildest dreams! Trips to Disneyland! Snorkeling in Hawaii!"

"Pony rides!" said Petunia.

"A new nonstick skillet!" said Mrs. Pepin.

"New insoles!" said Mr. Pepin.

"The kind of mac and cheese with a can of sauce in the box!" said Irving.

"And it's all thanks to you, Nelly," said Mr. Bradshaw, standing up and patting Nelly, who was quietly eating hay in the corner.

"Don't mention it," said Nelly, wishing they would all go home. There is only so much excitement a cow can stand.

The Pepins spent the rest of the evening dreaming about what they would do with their fortune. No one could wait until the next morning, when it was time to milk Nelly. Even Mr. Bradshaw awoke early for the big event.

"Don't be nervous," Mrs. Pepin told Nelly.

"We'll try not to stare," promised Irving.

"Stand back, everyone," said Nelly. "All right, Mr. Pepin, let 'er rip!"

Mr. Pepin sat down on the milking stool and giggled nervously. He began to milk. Then he stopped. He stared. Mrs. Pepin stared.

Irving pointed to the bottom of the milk bucket. "What's that?"

"I think . . ." began Petunia, "yes, I'm afraid it's milk."

"How odd," said Mr. Pepin.

" 'The heartache and the thousand natural shocks that flesh is heir to,' " said Mr. Bradshaw, who tended to quote *Hamlet* and generally overstate things when much excited.

"Nelly," said Mrs. Pepin reproachfully, "you're simply not trying."

"Oh dear," said Nelly, blushing.

Mr. Pepin began milking again, but soon it became evident that Nelly's lemonade days were over.

"I'm so sorry," said Nelly, shaking her head tearfully. "I'm afraid the lemonade was just a fluke."

Everyone gazed crestfallen at the milk.

Mrs. Pepin rallied first. "Don't worry, dear."

"Milk has calcium," said Irving helpfully.

"You can't make milk shakes with lemonade," added Petunia.

"I'm just an ordinary cow now," sobbed Nelly. "I could have been a somebody!"

"Now, Nelly," said Mr. Pepin, "you just keep up

those French and algebra lessons and forget the flash and instant celebrity this lemonade thing would have afforded. It's honest work that gets us through life, and you won't find that in a milk bucket."

The Pepins all nodded sagely, although Irving wistfully sneaked one last peek at the bucket just to be sure. While Mr. Pepin finished milking, everyone drifted tactfully out of the barn. Their dreams of riches died. "But," as Mrs. Pepin said on the way to the house, "a happy family already has as many riches as anyone can hope for."

"Except maybe for the occasional pony ride," said Petunia.

"And the kind of mac and cheese with a can of sauce in the box," said Irving.

•   •   •

That evening Mr. Bradshaw came to the Pepins' for dinner. They were all feeling rather chummy in their shared loss and were making jokes and jovial conversation over Mrs. Pepin's delicious clam chowder, when who should suddenly enter but a man wearing a top hat and tails and carrying an ebony cane. He eyed them specula-

tively and said, "Aha! Just as I thought." The mysterious stranger went into the kitchen, filled a bowl
with clam chowder, muscled Irving's and Petunia's
chairs apart to make room for his own, dipped a
spoon into his soup, and declared, "I have come
home!"

This was something of a conversation stopper.
The Pepins and their very fine neighbor Mr. Bradshaw looked at this dapper man in astonishment.
Who was he, and why was he insisting he was
home? The Pepins looked at one another wonder-
ingly. Was it possible that they had been sharing
their house with this gentleman all these years and
hadn't known it? Only you, dear reader, who have
proven yourself so vastly intelligent and discerning
in troubled times, can help me solve this, another
Pepin problem.

JUNEBUG
ARRIVES

Comments and speculations abound. And not a cheese doodle recipe in sight; gold stars for everyone! A reader from Good Hope, Georgia, says she certainly hopes the Pepins have not been sharing their house without knowing it. It's bad enough when there are ghosts. (If someone from Good Hope doesn't hope, does that mean that there are people in Normal who aren't?)

A reader from Yazoo City, Mississippi, says that he cannot count the number of times this has happened to him. Right now they are rounding up all the odds and ends of people scattered throughout the attic and moving them into nearby Panther Swamp. A town, asks your author? No, says the reader. A pleasant nature conservancy? Not exactly, says our reader, but a darn fine swamp. Mrs. Pepin protests that they have no Panther Swamp near Peony. That is just your tough luck, says this reader.

A reader from Nanafalia, Alabama, tries to say something, but by the time he has gotten out Nanafalia, Alabama, your author has fallen asleep. I'm terribly sorry, Nanafalia. Better luck next chapter.

Finally a reader from Skullbone, Tennessee, says that all southerners should stick together when it comes to odd people discovered living in one's home. In the first place, your author doesn't know what this means. In the second place, a reader from Low Moor, Virginia, says that she does not wish to be lumped in with all southerners, and thirdly, SKULLBONE? Who names these towns?

Mr. Bradshaw lifted his eyebrows. My, he thought, would the things that happen to these Pepins never stop surprising him?

"Are you Fred Astaire?" asked Petunia on a hunch.

"No," said the dapper gentleman, heading to the living room couch and picking up *The Peony Picayune*, Peony's only and best-selling newspaper, "I am not."

Mrs. Pepin went into the kitchen to get the chocolate cake and ice cream. What an etiquette problem this posed—do you offer strange people who barge into your house dessert?

The other Pepins watched Roy and Miranda circle the dapper gentleman warily, while Mrs. Pepin served her family and Mr. Bradshaw, absently spooning ice cream and cake into heaps on the table without the benefit of plates. Oh, she was rattled!

"Do you think," Mrs. Pepin asked meekly, making a desperate foray onto what appeared now to be the gentleman's turf, and peering over his newspaper, "that you could have made a mistake?"

"I *hardly* think that's likely! Do you?" said the gentleman with some asperity.

"My stars!" said Mrs. Pepin and scuttled back to the table, where the family were doing their best to eat the ice cream before it soaked into the tablecloth.

"Do you mean to tell me you don't know this gentleman?" hissed Mr. Bradshaw.

"Never saw him before in my life," hissed Mr. Pepin back.

"Well, I'll be darned," said Mr. Bradshaw. "Do you know, this is the first time something like this has ever happened to me."

"Something like what?" whispered Mrs. Pepin.

"A strange man walking in, declaring himself home, and picking up the evening paper."

"Well, it never happened to us before either," said Petunia. "Unless, that is, it happened to Mom and Dad before we were born." The Pepin children thought that Mr. and Mrs. Pepin had led exciting lives, possibly even as spies or avalanche patrollers, before giving birth to them.

"I really don't know what to do," declared Mrs. Pepin.

"Best to leave him there. Things will sort themselves out in time," said Mr. Pepin, who was a patient and philosophical man.

The Pepins and Mr. Bradshaw sneaked out to the porch with their evening coffee and lemonade. (For those of you who can remember way back to the second chapter and are even now leaping excitedly around, you can just calm right down because this lemonade came from the grocery store and not Nelly and is not the same thing at all.) They rocked on the porch and watched the sunset. Mr. Bradshaw yawned finally and said he guessed he had better go home, as he was going to have a busy day tomorrow at Bradshaw's Unusual and Extraordinary Snack Products. The company was trying to create edible pencils that children could suck when they got stuck on a particularly sticky math problem.

"But that's the trouble," said Mr. Bradshaw with a sigh. "The stickiness. We all know that children like to store pencils behind their ears."

"Yes, of course you're right," said Irving, currently sporting six or seven.

"Indeed," said Mr. Bradshaw. "And our experimental edible pencils get extremely sticky and attach themselves to people's hair. Parents won't like it. Not one little bit. The trick is to make a healthy edible pencil that won't get sticky but that children like. I thought perhaps a carrot base?"

"Yuck," said Petunia.

"Ish," said Irving.

"Ah, you see," said Mr. Bradshaw, standing up and taking his leave. He hung his head, shook it sadly, and walked slowly home. Many children think life is easy for those in the world of snack products. It is not.

The Pepins went in. The dapper gentleman was still in the living room. He was snoring. Mr. Pepin peered over the newspaper, which had come to rest on the dapper gentleman's face.

"I guess he's spending the night," Mr. Pepin said.

"Ah," said Mrs. Pepin. They tiptoed off to bed.

The next day when Petunia and Irving returned from school, the dapper gentleman was sitting on the front porch.

"No, I know what you're thinking," said Mrs. Pepin, who was dusting. "But I had to move him. It's vacuuming day, and he just couldn't hang out any longer in the living room."

"Yes, and yet," said Petunia, "I don't know how good he looks on the porch."

"It's the top hat," said Irving. "People around

here just don't sit on their front porches in top hats."

"Do you suppose we could ask him to switch it with one of your father's fedoras?" asked Mrs. Pepin.

They were rather shy about talking to the dapper gentleman after he had barked at them the day before, but they saw no other way.

Petunia went out on the porch, her father's fedora in her trembling hand.

"Please, sir, do you mind changing hats?" she asked.

"Do I look like I'm married to this hat?" asked the gentleman, whipping off his top hat and donning the fedora.

Mrs. Pepin, Irving, and Petunia sighed with relief and went to the front walk to survey him critically.

"It doesn't do much for his skin tone," said Petunia finally.

"Let's try a beret," said Mrs. Pepin.

The Pepins tried a beret, a ski cap, Mrs. Pepin's sunbonnet (definitely not), a baseball hat, and assorted toques.

"Well, really," said Mrs. Pepin, "I think he looks better with no hat at all, but let's leave the red toque on him."

"Let's let Dad decide when he gets home from work," said Irving.

When Mr. Pepin got home, it was *his* opinion that the problem with the dapper gentleman wasn't his head apparel; it was his location.

"He's not a porch dapper gentleman," said Mr. Pepin. "You can see that at once. Let's try moving him into the library."

The Pepins kept him in the library for twenty-four hours, but there wasn't a chair that really showed him off adequately. They tried perching him on the mantel in the den, but his legs blocked the fireplace. He had long legs. He had extremely long legs.

"Almost freakish," whispered Mrs. Pepin as she watched them gently swing in front of the fireplace grate.

"Now, dear," admonished Mr. Pepin.

They put him in the bathroom—well, you can imagine how satisfactory that was. They put him in the pantry among the cans and jars, but he was really quite a bit overdressed for that. They put him in the birdbath, hoping against hope he would blossom as a garden ornament. Finally, in desperation, as they were shoving him into the attic, they spied some old family photos.

"Wait a minute here," said Irving. "Can this be?

But how extraordinary. What is the dapper gentleman doing in this photo?"

Everyone crowded around the old picture in its tarnished silver frame.

"Good lord," said Mrs. Pepin. "It is he!"

"Why yes, the very same but much younger. He's Bartholomew William Culbert Pepin: the Long-Lost Pepin!" exclaimed Mr. Pepin.

"Yes indeed," said the Long-Lost Pepin, who had apparently just been waiting for someone to recognize him. He brushed a dust mote off his shoulder imperturbably, because, you see, his breeding was such that he never shed a bead of sweat or wrinkled his exquisite brow, even under the trying circumstance of being moved bodily from room to room. "I have come home."

"Welcome home, Long-Lost Pepin!" said Mr. Pepin.

The family trooped downstairs, Mr. B.W.C. Pepin included, to eat tea cakes and hear the story of how he was misplaced at a family wedding and ended up (fantastically) in Borneo, from which extreme location he had to make his way home, wearing top hat and tails.

"Well, I think after such a journey as that, we must ask you to join us for dinner!" said Mrs. Pepin.

"Thank you," said Bartholomew William Culbert Pepin. "I admit to being a tad peckish. My wife, as you may or may not know, had the misfortune of being misplaced with me, also ending up in Borneo, also having to make her way home. She should be here any day."

"What is taking her so long?" asked Petunia.

"She is wearing heels," said the Long-Lost Pepin.

Eventually, Mrs. Bartholomew William Culbert Pepin, also known as Junebug, arrived with many runs in her nylons. The Pepins had yet another welcoming feast. Mr. B.W.C. Pepin made a speech. He thanked the Pepins for their hospitality. "And now," he continued, "I will tell you why I have come."

"Oh, do," said Mrs. Pepin.

"All ears," said Mr. Pepin.

"Explanations are always so nice," said Petunia.

"Ever curious," said Irving.

"I have come," said the Long-Lost Pepin after a dramatic pause, "to solve all your problems."

"You mean this is the end of the Pepins' problems?" asked Mr. Pepin in complete astonishment.

"Yes," said Mr. B.W.C. Pepin, "it is."

Junebug nodded and ate her fourth piece of pie.

Yes, dear reader, that's it. The book is over. Or is it? How perspicacious are you?

THE
Mysterious
Envelope

Indeed, you are very perspicacious. You have continued to turn pages because not for one instant did you believe the rest of these pages were blank. Yes, it was all a diversion because your author wanted to waddle into the kitchen and cut herself another piece of spice cake with chocolate frosting. It is not for nothing that your author invents Long-Lost characters. It is to Mr. B.W.C. Pepin and his wife, Junebug, that we now return. But first we must hear what the readers have to say about this being the end to the Pepins' problems.

Naturally, what I am hearing foremost is the sound of children all across North America screaming in pain at the thought of no more Pepin problems. This cannot be the end of the Pepins' problems, thinks a reader from Mesita, New Mexico. We are only on page 56. A good point.

Give us your editor, demands a reader from Boring, Maryland. Alas, your author's editor is seldom available. She is so desperately beautiful that, despite herself, the office staff is always entering her in beauty contests so that she is never around, she is trotting up and down stages wearing roses and crowns and such. It's a curse.

A reader from Bohemia, Louisiana is . . . what? Is closing her book? No! Wait! Too late. She is taking it back to the library. Some readers will believe anything the author says. But the rest of you who can hardly believe this is the end of the Pepins' problems, read on, read on.

Like many affectionately welcomed houseguests, Mr. B.W.C. Pepin and Junebug arrived unannounced, made themselves immediately at home, stayed for three years (during which time the children aged not one iota—odd, isn't it?), ate everything in sight, and then departed quite suddenly with no explanation, leaving behind no trace of their existence except for a few cracker crumbs and several hundred dollars' worth of phone bills.

"My heavens," said Mrs. Pepin. "I do not see how we can go on. I was so used to the Long-Lost Pepin solving my every dilemma."

"And Junebug hoovering the toast crumbs off the dining room rug with her nose," added Mr. Pepin.

"It was quite a talent," said Irving, the sixth-grade genius.

"I personally shall relish not having to share my kibble with the ever-hoovering Junebug," said Roy, who had learned to talk in the interval between chapters. And why not? What else had he to do with his time?

"Perhaps we shall have no problems," said Mrs. Pepin in her hopeful, quavering way.

"Perhaps we should not live in a fool's paradise," said Miranda, who had also learned to talk but generally chose not to, although when she did, she could be rather cutting.

"Perhaps we should go sit in a dark closet immediately in the hope that the problems will not find us," said Petunia.

And so that's where Mr. Bradshaw found them several hours later. An industrious spider had already woven a tangled web about the family and was hanging from Irving's nose when Mr. Bradshaw, who had come over to borrow a tennis racket for his evening exercise with the Pepins' cow, Nelly, opened the door.

"Greetings," said Mr. Bradshaw. "Might I venture that you have been here for some time?"

"Several hours," said Mr. Pepin.

"Ah, then that explains why you have not yet received this. I found it shoved under your front door," said Mr. Bradshaw, handing Mr. Pepin a large square envelope.

"Why, what is it?" asked Mrs. Pepin.

"It appears to be a missive of some sort," replied Mr. Pepin, handling it gingerly.

"Unless," said Petunia, "it is a cleverly disguised pony. Has someone, knowing my birthday is only eight months away, bought me a pony?" Dear reader, no one had.

"Just as I thought," said Irving. "Our problems find us even in dark closets."

"I'm just happy not to share my kibble," said Roy, who, though he had learned to speak, sometimes had a dearth of things to say. Excuse me for editorializing, but you, dear reader, might consider this the next time you wish your dog could talk.

"Perhaps it isn't a problem," said Petunia. "Perhaps it's that nice Mr. McMahon with a check for several million dollars."

"Do you think that nice Mr. McMahon could fit in such a small space?" asked Mrs. Pepin, eyeing the envelope warily.

"You don't think it's explosive, do you?" Mr. Pepin asked Mr. Bradshaw. (Mr. Bradshaw had been on a bomb squad during the war, and the Pepins took all their unexploded watermelons and summer squashes to him for examination.)

Mr. Bradshaw took the envelope and held it carefully by two corners. "It does not appear to be explosive," he said, "but we cannot be too careful. The first line of defense is to douse it in water. If we give it a thorough dousing, it is almost sure not to explode."

All the Pepins, Mr. Bradshaw, and the spider, who had developed a spectator interest, trooped out of the closet and gathered in the kitchen. Mr. Bradshaw continued to hold the potentially explosive envelope while Mrs. Pepin turned on the tap.

No water came out. "How it does remind me of the time Nelly gave lemonade instead of milk," said Mrs. Pepin nostalgically.

"Ah yes," said Mr. Pepin. "That was during our cheesemaking phase."

"Now what?" asked Mrs. Pepin.

"Perhaps we should all blow on it," suggested Petunia. Everyone blew hopefully on the envelope. It did not go off, but Mr. Bradshaw deemed this inconclusive.

"What about some eau de cologne?" he suggested. "A good dousing of eau de cologne seriously does something or other."

"And it's so much fun to work the atomizer!" agreed Petunia.

Mrs. Pepin got her bottle of Chanel Number Five, and they atomized like mad. Then for good measure, the Pepins did a rain dance in their underwear. It had nothing to do with the letter—it was just something they hadn't done in a while.

"Now," said Mrs. Pepin, picking up the perfumed envelope, "I shall open it."

"Stop!" cried Petunia and Irving.

"Why?" cried Mrs. Pepin, dropping the envelope in haste.

"If it is our problems finding us again," said Irving, "and you don't open it, then we'll have foiled them."

"Without the Long-Lost Pepin. Without even Junebug," added Petunia.

"And without having to share my kibble," said Roy.

"Yes," said Mr. Pepin, "but if it isn't our problems, if for instance it is a large check from Mr. McMahon or a similarly public-spirited benefactor, we shall never know. We shall go unriched."

"Unriched?" said Mr. Bradshaw.

"Mr. Pepin has a way with words," said Mrs. Pepin.

All nodded solemnly. In the end they could not agree what to do. They debated the issue by day. They debated the issue by night. They debated it in dark closets and on sunny porches, in fields, in streams, and (in memory of Junebug) while hoovering crumbs off the floor with their noses. All that they could agree upon was that you, dear reader, must be asked for your helpful, intelligent, and insightful advice and speculations, and that dogs have so little to call their own, they really should not have to put up with people nosing around in their kibble.

the Other VERY Fine NEIGHBOR

Ah, you dear readers, always so happy to share your ideas.

A reader from Croton-on-Hudson, New York (where they *do* believe in prepositions), thinks the Pepins should fly to Hollywood, find Mr. McMahon, and ask him in a friendly, disinterested sort of way if he'd sent them any mail recently.

A reader from Delight, Arkansas, says that perhaps the Pepins are not aware of all the craft uses for mail. You can shellac it and use it as a doorstop, or sew it all together and make a mail quilt, or trim it in red and green rickrack and hang it on the Christmas tree.

Another reader, from Lone Elm, Kansas, says that there in Lone Elm they don't believe in opening envelopes. Instead they take all their envelopes and put them unopened in a big Dumpster under the lone elm and once a year burn them up and have a wienie roast while singing "Kumbaya."

Someone else, from Smoke Signal, Arizona, suggests that the Pepins might feed their mysterious envelope to a goat and see what happens. It appears that this dear reader's goats eat anything and consequently get fed a lot of junk mail. But the Pepins have no goats, and Nelly is far too dignified to eat junk mail. Why, in fact, she protests, she doesn't even read the stuff! In the end, the Pepins simply went next door to Miss Hermione Poopenstat's. She had lived next to the Pepins for many years, but they had yet to meet her.

When Miss Poopenstat answered the door, she said, "Ah, I see you have the mail I forwarded to you," and proceeded to solve the Pepins' problem by ripping it open herself. It did not explode. It did not even fizzle. Instead, inside was a slightly soggy postcard from Junebug saying she and her husband, the Long-Lost Pepin, were having a delightful, if chilly, time dancing under the northern lights in Helsinki. She had Scotch-taped a few toast crumbs to the postcard for old times' sake.

"You see," said Miss Poopenstat, "I received the incorrectly addressed postcard with my mail, and having once been a U.S. postmistress, I knew the importance of putting it in a proper envelope and redirecting it by hand. Fortunately, you only live next door. If I had had to return it to Helsinki with a TRY TO GET THE ADDRESS RIGHT NEXT TIME, HONEY rubber stamp, it would have taken me much longer. When I retired, I kept all my postal stamps."

The Pepins apologized for being so much trouble, and then they all trooped inside (along with Roy and Miranda and their very fine neighbor Mr. Bradshaw). Miss Poopenstat made them hot chocolate, and they sat around her kitchen table waiting for it to be cool enough to sip.

"Dear lady," said Mr. Pepin, "I am sorry to have taken so long to make your acquaintance. The fact of the matter is that we had had so much luck with our neighbor to the left, our very fine neighbor Mr. Bradshaw, whom you see before you, that we had no hope of having equal luck with the neighbor to the right. In fact, Irving feared you must be evil."

Miss Poopenstat put her hand to her heart. "Evil? *Moi*?"

"It stands to reason," said Irving. "For the balance, you know. Good neighbor on one side, evil on the other. I am taking physics, even though I am only in the sixth grade."

"He's a genius," whispered Mrs. Pepin proudly.

"And I can assure you that what you learn in physics is that everything is balanced," said Irving. "Well, that, and that if you could run fast enough, you could jump through the slot in a mailbox. I assure you, that is simply a fact."

"And can you run that fast?" asked Miss Poopenstat.

"No one can run that fast," said Irving.

"Why don't you try?" suggested Miss Poopenstat sweetly.

"Yes, well, the point is that everything is balanced," said Irving.

"An infectious carbuncle is not balanced," said Miss Poopenstat.

"No, that is true," said Irving.

"A banana is just a banana," said Miss Poopenstat.

"Let's change the subject," said Petunia.

"I know," said Miss Poopenstat. "Let's examine my postal rubber stamps."

The Pepins and Miss Poopenstat and their very fine neighbor Mr. Bradshaw tripped upstairs to the attic, and Miss Poopenstat got out her large box of postal stamps and her stamp pad. She stamped all the Pepins' foreheads, and each person had to guess what was stamped on his or her own forehead from clues given by others.

"Ah, such a delightful game. I used to play it on rainy days in the attic with my cats. Of course," said Miss Poopenstat musingly, "it is difficult to read what is stamped on fur."

"Now she tells me," said Miranda.

In the end they deciphered all the forehead messages. Petunia's read, I AM NOT DELIVERING THIS UNTIL YOU LEARN TO PRINT CLEARLY. Irving's said, DO NOT EXPECT RETURN MAIL. THIS IS A

CEMETERY. Mr. Bradshaw's said, YOUR HOUSE NEEDS REPAINTING.

"I took that one along with me on my delivery rounds to stamp on people's doors," said Miss Poopenstat. "You have no idea how dreary it is to deliver mail every day to the same houses with their peeling paint and unswept walkways. Well, you do have to draw the line somewhere." She whispered this last to Mrs. Pepin.

Mr. Pepin's forehead read, STOP SENDING IN FOR ALL THESE HEAVY CATALOGS. YOUR POSTAL EM-PLOYEE IS BREAKING HER BACK, AND I BET YOU DON'T EVEN ORDER ANYTHING FROM THEM. I BET YOU JUST LIKE READING THEM IN THE BATHTUB.

"I never had any luck with that one," whispered Miss Poopenstat to Mrs. Pepin. "People who like catalogs are just fanatic."

"I like to read catalogs in the bathtub," confessed Mrs. Pepin.

"So do I!" said Miss Poopenstat. "That's why it was so deliciously sinful to stamp it on other people's catalogs!" She and Mrs. Pepin giggled diabolically.

Miranda put a paw delicately on her forehead. "What nonsense," she whispered to Roy. "Anybody knows you don't send for catalogs; they find you and tell all their friends."

Mrs. Pepin's forehead stamp read, IF YOU DON'T WANT YOUR POSTAL WORKER TO READ YOUR POSTCARDS, YOU SHOULD PUT THEM IN ENVELOPES. WE'RE ONLY HUMAN, YOU KNOW. Miranda's stamp read, FOR HEAVEN'S SAKE STOP SENDING CARDS TO THIS NEW BABY.

"I saved that for houses where I knew there'd been a new arrival. I like children, Lord knows I like children, I just don't think they should be allowed to get mail," said Miss Poopenstat.

"I see," said Mr. Pepin. "And just what kind of mail do you approve of?"

"Electronic mail!" said Miss Poopenstat and fell over laughing with Mrs. Pepin again.

"I think Mommy has found a friend," said Petunia to Irving, and everyone crept back downstairs, leaving Mrs. Pepin and Miss Poopenstat madly exchanging recipes and pounding the floor in mirth.

When Mrs. Pepin and Miss Poopenstat came downstairs ten minutes later, they were both rather red in the face but quite jolly still. Roy was racing around chasing Miranda, who had told him what was stamped on his forehead before he had a chance to guess. That Miranda!

"Yes," said Miss Poopenstat, reading Roy's forehead wistfully. It read, IGNORE YOUR BILLS AND MAYBE THEY'LL STOP SENDING THEM. "When I was a United States postal employee, I could have anything I liked made into a rubber stamp. That's the law."

"I wish someone would have a rubber stamp made that said, DON'T GROW PURPLE RHODO-DENDRONS. I do despise those liverish-looking shrubs," said Mr. Bradshaw, trying to join in politely.

But Miss Poopenstat was not at all welcoming. "How very peculiar. You must be a very peculiar man. Petulant. Touchy. He must be difficult to have for a neighbor," she said, turning to Mrs. Pepin. "Not like me."

"You are both very fine neighbors," said Mr.

Pepin, trying to smooth things over but getting sour looks from both of them.

"Ah!" said Petunia. "We haven't had our hot chocolate!"

Everyone reached gratefully for the cups, gliding by the awkward moment. They each picked one up and took a sip. The hot chocolate was cold.

They all lowered their cups and stared mournfully into them.

"I don't like cold hot chocolate," said Miss Poopenstat.

"Perhaps we should think of it as chocolate milk," said Petunia.

"Perhaps we should make a rubber stamp for you that reads, PERKY CHILDREN MAKE EXCELLENT DOORSTOPS," said Miss Poopenstat.

"I think she is the evil neighbor after all," whispered Irving to his sister.

"Thank you for your support," whispered Petunia, and the two of them crawled under the table to await further developments.

"Well, I don't know what to do. I can't drink

this slop!" said Miss Poopenstat, setting it down emphatically.

"Perhaps the thing to do is to make it hot again," said Mrs. Pepin.

"Well, clearly, dear, you haven't been living in a storm cellar your whole life. Tell on, tell on," said Miss Poopenstat. It was becoming clear that Mrs. Pepin was the only one out of the whole group whom she liked.

"I'm afraid that's as far as my limited imagination takes me," replied Mrs. Pepin. "I know how to make cold milk into hot chocolate, but I'm afraid I don't know how to make hot chocolate that has gotten cold hot again."

"It's a conundrum," said Miss Poopenstat.

"Well, I don't know about that—" began Mr. Bradshaw.

"It's a conundrum wrapped in an enigma swallowed by a maze," snapped Miss Poopenstat. "And furthermore, *I'm* the very fine neighbor. You, sir, are an aardvark."

Mr. Bradshaw, who had never been called an aardvark before, crept under the table with Petunia and Irving.

"I do not know what to do," said Miss Poopenstat. "I offered you hot chocolate, and now I find myself unable to give you hot chocolate. It is at best inhospitable."

"What is it at worst?" asked Irving from under the table.

"I am going to have a rubber stamp made up," said Miss Poopenstat ruminatively, "that reads, LITTLE CHILDREN WHO DWELL UNDER TABLES SHOULD HAVE BLUE CHEESE MASHED IN THEIR HAIR."

"She really *is* the evil neighbor," whispered Petunia.

"You would never catch me threatening to mash blue cheese into your hair," whispered Mr. Bradshaw. "Cheddar perhaps."

"There is a solution for everything, I always find," said Mr. Pepin. "At least, that has been my very long experience with problems."

"Why don't you join your friends under the table?" said Miss Poopenstat. "I hear they are starting a game of bridge and need a fourth."

Mr. Pepin took the hint and dove beneath the oilcloth.

Mrs. Pepin and Miss Poopenstat were therefore free to brainstorm the matter of the cold hot chocolate themselves, but as the hours passed, they felt that their efforts were not to be rewarded, and so, dear reader, I put it to you: How can the Pepins and their neighbors restore the hot that is truly the essence of hot chocolate?

the Mouse Squisher

Fortunately, dear readers have taken the matter to heart. Many have gotten out of bed, slipped downstairs to the kitchen, and made themselves hot chocolate to let cool and then experiment with reheating. Just a sip, thinks the reader in Zigzag, Oregon. The merest taste, thinks a reader in East or perhaps it was West Braintree, Vermont. But before they knew it, that experimental hot chocolate was gone. There are some readers who should give up science as a career goal.

Our dear reader in Reepsville, North Carolina,

suggests that hot was hot because molecules were racing around very quickly, and if Petunia would only run around the house six or seven times carrying a mug of cold chocolate, it would speed up the molecules and heat up the drink. Petunia thought this was a fine idea. She took her mug and raced around the living room, leaping over couches and bric-a-brac.

"Now try leaping through the slot in a mailbox!" Miss Poopenstat urged.

"What?" asked Petunia, turning to look at Miss Poopenstat and tripping over the coffee table. The hot chocolate ended up on Miss Poopenstat's fine Argentinian rug.

They all decided to take their mugs outside after that and wait for more readers to respond.

Wait! Yes, my antennae quiver. One dear reader from Brookline, Massachusetts, thinks that all the Pepins need to do is to find a very successful writer and have him or her blow some hot air on the cold chocolate.

"I think that's a very distasteful idea," said Mrs. Pepin.

"All those germs," agreed their very fine neighbor Mr. Bradshaw.

"Does this imply that very successful writers are full of hot air?" asked Petunia. "Why, all of the successful writers I have ever known have been famous for helping the indolent, the indigent, and the ignorant. They are full of the milk of human kindness and every other virtue you can possibly think of, and should be sent money by large corporations in appreciation of their good works. Even unsuccessful writers are so wonderful that I can barely stand to speak of them."

Dear reader, how perceptive Petunia has become. Truly main character material!

All the Pepins and their very fine neighbor Mr. Bradshaw bowed their heads for a moment, thinking reverently of writers everywhere. Then they moved on to more interesting things.

"It seems," said Mr. Bradshaw, "that I will just have to invent something!"

"Get out of here!" said Miss Poopenstat.

"He does invent things," whispered Mrs. Pepin in Miss Poopenstat's ear. "He owns and is the president of Bradshaw's Unusual and Extraordinary Snack Products, makers of the edible lightbulb."

"Humph!" said Miss Poopenstat.

"Whatever is it, dear?" asked Mrs. Pepin. "Do you not like snacks?"

"I've tried those edible lightbulbs," said Miss Poopenstat. "I once bought a large box of them and put them in every light fixture in the house. The next night, getting rather munchy while watching Martha Stewart—the way one does, you know—I roamed from room to room eating them. Finally, when there was just the dim light of the bulb hanging over the basement stairs, I had to make a decision: Do I want to be able to see, or do I want to satisfy my snacking needs? So I reached up, gobble gobble gobble, was cast into

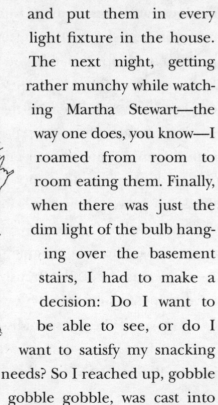

total darkness, and fell down the basement stairs."

"Goodness," said Mrs. Pepin. "Did you break a leg?"

"No, but I got chutney all over my night-gown."

"Chutney?"

"Must you ask? Can there be no mysteries?"

The Pepins and Mr. Bradshaw were listening politely to this conversation. Roy and Miranda had gone home. They often wondered why they had bothered learning to talk. It seemed to them that people seldom had anything sensible to say.

"Well!" said Mr. Pepin. "I'm sure we all have our snack product preferences. I personally always find it nice to be sitting next to a table lamp, feel a bit peckish, and discover a snack product ready to be unscrewed. But that's just me. I think, though, that if our very fine neighbor offers to invent something to make cold hot chocolate hot again, we should take him up on it."

"Hogwash," said Miss Poopenstat.

"All in favor, say aye," said Mr. Pepin. Everyone said aye but Miss Poopenstat, who said, "I don't," and thought she was being very witty.

Miss Poopenstat sat down on her porch and said she was going to stay there until her hot chocolate rehotted itself through the power of positive thinking. And so they left her, sitting and staring into her cup, thinking positive thoughts as hard as she could.

The Pepins were very excited to be invited to see Mr. Bradshaw's home laboratory, where he did his preliminary inventions before taking them to the factory. The Pepins had never been inside his laboratory before.

"My goodness," said Mr. Pepin, gazing at the beakers full of purple cottage cheese.

"This looks like a kitchen," said Mrs. Pepin.

"It looks like a kitchen crossed with a mad scientist's laboratory," said Irving.

"Who are you calling mad, little boy? BROU-HAHA!" said Mr. Bradshaw, donning a black cape. "Why, there's nothing mad about it! Is that a turnip I see walking across the ceiling?"

"No, it's a salamander," said Petunia.

"No, I believe it's a chameleon," said Irving.

"Ah, the LIZARDS ARE LOOSE!" shouted Mr. Bradshaw. "I hate it when that happens."

"Does it happen often?"
asked Mrs. Pepin,
looking warily at
her feet to see if
anything was slithering
across the floor.

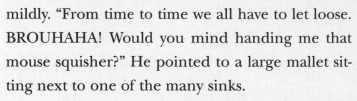

"From time to time,"
said Mr. Bradshaw
mildly. "From time to time we all have to let loose.
BROUHAHA! Would you mind handing me that
mouse squisher?" He pointed to a large mallet sitting next to one of the many sinks.

"Oh dear," said Petunia.
"You don't really squish mice
with that thing, do you?"

"Certainly not," said
Mr. Bradshaw. "What kind
of a beast do you take me
for? No, it's called a
mouse squisher because
my mice laboratory assis-
tants, Max and Arnold,
use it to squish things
for me. Max! Max!"

called Mr. Bradshaw. A mouse dashed across the counter, took the mallet from Mr. Bradshaw, and proceeded to squish all the things Mr. Bradshaw was throwing into a large mixing bowl. "Let's see," he muttered, "two tennis balls, one Ping-Pong paddle, a large, dirty gray sock, fourteen breath mints, nine holes of golf, and a six-pack of nationally advertised fizzy beverage. That should do it."

Max was hopping up and down, beating things for all he was worth. He worked so hard that sweat dripped from his brow and made a little puddle on the counter by his feet.

"Don't mind that," said Mr. Bradshaw. "The lizards lick it up."

"I think I'm going to be sick," said Petunia.

"Science is not for all stomachs," said Mr. Bradshaw. "Pity. Now we will take this mixture and put it into the cooker and see what happens."

Mr. Bradshaw took the mixing bowl over to a

large contraption with many doors and chutes and poured the mixture in. Then he pressed a button, and the machine vibrated noisily while the mouse took a nap.

"We mustn't stop the machine until Max wakes up," said Mr. Bradshaw.

"Really? Extraordinary," said Mr. Pepin, who found the whole process of inventing fascinating.

"Is that how you time the cooking process?"

"No, Max finds the noise soothing and it helps him sleep. Dreadful case of insomnia, this mouse. Can only sleep with the cooker on."

They stood around and watched the mouse snore for several minutes, and then Mr. Bradshaw said, "Well, this is certainly boring. Although not as boring as when I used to have to rock him to sleep with lullabies for hours on end. Ah, how nurturing is a double-edged sword."

Mr. Bradshaw turned off the machine and Max woke up, squeaked irritably, and ran into a hole. "Rodents," whispered Mr. Bradshaw confidentially to Mrs. Pepin, "can't live with them, can't live without them. Well then, let's see what we've got here." He opened a door at the bottom of the contraption, much like the little flap of metal on a gumball machine, and out popped several pellets.

"These should hotten up your drinks, yes siree, I can tell just by looking at them!" said Mr. Bradshaw. "Shall we take them over to Miss Poopen-stat's and try them out and perhaps even gloat a bit?"

The Pepins regarded the pellets with a certain amount of distaste. How difficult it is to drop dirty gray socks into one's beverage, even if they're mixed with tennis balls.

"But science marches on!" said Mrs. Pepin, and they all agreed that this was so. Off they trot-ted to Miss Poopenstat's. On the way they ran into Miranda, explained what they were about to do in the name of science, and asked her to come along.

"I think not," said Miranda, and she went to have a good chuckle with Roy about it.

Miss Poopenstat was still sitting on the porch staring at her hot chocolate, but when she saw Mr. Bradshaw returning, she gulped it down.

"How goes it with the positive thinking?" he asked.

"Fine and dandy, yes, my hot chocolate got hot just this second. It got smoking hot, steaming hot, so hot it almost melted the cup," said Miss Poopen-stat. "It positively burned my tongue. No, I shan't eat for a week."

"Ah, what a successful day we are having, then, my good lady!" said Mr. Bradshaw. "Because the Pepins and I have invented an edible pellet that reheats cold drinks."

"Oh no no," said the Pepins, rubbing their toes modestly in the grass. "You did all the inventing."

"You are too kind," said Mr. Bradshaw.

"No, you are too kind," said the Pepins.

"Oh no no, you are too kind," said Mr. Bradshaw.

"Oh, get on with it—I don't believe you invented anything of the sort," said Miss Poopenstat.

"Allow us to demonstrate," said Mr. Bradshaw. "One, two, three!" The Pepins dropped their pellets into their cups. Immediately steam arose, and they gave a loud cheer.

"Another successful invention!" said Mr. Bradshaw proudly. "And now you must all drink your hot chocolate to celebrate!"

BRADSHAW'S

Edible Hot Pellets

The Pepins hesitated. They raised their cups and were about to take a sip when Petunia said, "I know! Let's see if hot chocolate makes grass grow faster."

"I'm almost sure it would," agreed Irving, and they hastily poured their hot chocolate on Miss Poopenstat's lawn.

Nothing happened. "Try, try again," said Mr. and Mrs. Pepin, and they poured out their hot chocolate as well.

Mr. Bradshaw had no hot chocolate. He had given his to Petunia when she spilled hers. "I see you have the souls of inventors, every one of you!" he said proudly.

"It is you, our very fine neighbor, who have taught us the meaning of experimentation," said Mrs. Pepin.

"Your very fine neighbor indeed," said Miss Poopenstat, rising and collecting all the cups. "*I* am the very fine neighbor. This man is an impostor. This man is an aardvark."

"Excuse me, dear lady," said Mr. Bradshaw. "But I have been the very fine neighbor since the first chapter and have not once been described by the author as an aardvark. *You* are the impostor."

"Well," said Miss Poopenstat to the Pepins, "who is the very fine neighbor? I'm sure you can tell just by looking."

But the Pepins couldn't. They looked and they looked. They looked until the sun went down and the stars came out, but Mr. Bradshaw and Miss Poopenstat exhibited no visible signs.

"This is truly dreadful," said Mrs. Pepin. "Shouldn't we, the Pepins, be able to tell at a glance?"

"It isn't dreadful, dear," said Mr. Pepin, putting a consolatory arm around his wife's weary shoulders. "It is merely another problem, and thank heaven we have a way to solve it."

"Our readers!" said Irving.

"Our dear readers!" said Petunia.

"Our dear dear readers!" said all the Pepins, and they did a little Portuguese scarf dance in the balmy twilight.

the VERY Fine NEIGHBOR-OFF

Forgive me if I did not hear your solution. All this talk of balmy twilight air sent your author running straight to Florida, where she was seen cavorting on the beach with some pink flamingos and a gentleman she nicknamed Miami Toots. But all vacations must end. How we all cry boo-hoo, boo-hoo when a new chapter is not immediately forthcoming. So off with my sunglasses and on with some of your delightful solutions.

A reader in Hanover, New Hampshire, thinks that the Pepins should turn both neighbors upside down and shake them hard to see what falls out of their pockets. She does not explain exactly how this will prove who is the very fine neighbor, but perhaps this is obvious to you, dear reader, and it is only your author who is a little dim.

Another reader from Peanut, California, says that the Pepins should put Mr. Bradshaw and Miss Poopenstat next to a horse and see who sounds most like it. This puzzled your author until she realized that this reader had misunderstood and thought the Pepins were looking for a very fine *neigher*. Perhaps next chapter.

In the end it was a reader from Stamping Ground, Kentucky, who came up with the best solution (and also a recipe for best-ever brownies) and won the prize. "A PRIZE?" I hear you say. "I didn't know there was a prize." "What was the prize?" "I would have thought a solution in your direction if I'd known there was a prize."

Well, there is no prize, but your author certainly knows how to get your attention. This brownie-baking Kentuckian suggested that the Pepins have a Neighbor-Off, sort of along the lines of the Pillsbury Bake-Off.

"What a delightful solution," said Mrs. Pepin.

The Pepins spent a week trying to think of events in which Mr. Bradshaw and Miss Poopenstat could compete. It was finally decided that there would be five: The Shoveling-Snow-off-the-Whole-Sidewalk-Even-Though-Some-of-It-Runs-Past-Your-Neighbor's-House Event, the Chicken-Soup-Delivery-to-the-Sick Event, the Buying-of-Girl-Scout-Cookies-and-Raffle-Tickets-and-Magazine-Subscriptions-from-Neighboring-Children Event, the Return-of-the-Injured-Pet Event, the Cheerful-Greeting-As-You-Pass-Them-Sitting-on-Their-Porch-of-an-Evening Event.

The Pepins carefully explained all these categories to the contestants, who wrote them down with feverish, puckered brows and went home to practice for a week. Miss Poopenstat was almost disqualified when it was discovered that she was getting professional coaching.

"Miss Poopenstat! This is an amateur event!" said Mr. Pepin, looking shocked.

"Drat!" said Miss Poopenstat and stomped into her house.

Mr. Bradshaw simply went about his normal work, shuttling between his laboratory and his factory, creating unusual snack products with the help of his lab assistant mice, Max and Arnold. He practiced only when he could spare time from candy-striping and his volunteer work at the hospice.

At week's end the Pepins set up a starting gate. "Now, when you finish one event, you collect a ribbon and go on to the next. The first person to complete all five events wins," said Irving.

"That would be me," said Miss Poopenstat.

"And the one to come in second," said Irving, frowning slightly, "is an aardvark."

"Why does either one of them have to be an aardvark?" asked Roy, turning to Miranda. "That's what I'd like to know."

Miranda shrugged as best she could in her sling. Both she and Roy were wearing phony bandages to play their parts in Event Number Four, the Return-of-the-Injured-Pet.

Mrs. Pepin held the starter pistol, and Mr. Bradshaw and Miss Poopenstat huddled at the starting gate. Miss Poopenstat, fearing that Mr.

Bradshaw had a toe placed ahead of her own little piggy, elbowed him sharply in the ribs. Mr. Bradshaw jumped back. "After you, dear lady," he said.

"On your mark. Get set . . ." began Mrs. Pepin (who, like many of us, had always wanted to say that), when suddenly a crowd appeared down the street and marched right up to the starting gate. They were wearing gym shorts and sweatsuits and running shoes.

"Whatever can this be?" asked Mrs. Pepin.

"We want to enter the Neighbor-Off," said one woman. "We're neighbors, too, after all."

"Not next-door neighbors," said Miss Poopenstat. "I say to heck with them and get out of the way."

"*Au contraire,* the more the merrier," said Mr. Bradshaw, trying to make room for them at the narrow starting gate, while Miss Poopenstat beat them back with cupped hands.

"Yes, they should all have an opportunity to win the large cash prize," said the author from somewhere in the clouds.

"A CASH PRIZE?" said Mr. Bradshaw and Miss

Poopenstat together. "There's a CASH PRIZE?"

"No, I was just messing with your heads," said the voice from the clouds.

"Twice?" said Mr. Bradshaw. "In one chapter?"

"Let's get on with it," said Mr. Quinn, who lived across the street and appeared many chapters back.

"On your mark. Get set . . ." said Mrs. Pepin. "Go!"

And they were off! Like chargers they flew toward Event Number One—the Shoveling-Snow-off-the-Whole-Sidewalk-Even-Though-Some-of-It-Runs-Past-Your-Neighbor's-House Event. There was no snow on the sidewalks, so the neighbors had to pantomime. One poor woman got frostbite and had to be carried to a waiting ambulance. Another slipped on the imaginary ice and was nearly trampled, but Mr. Bradshaw helped her up and sat with her until she felt herself again, by which time Miss Poopenstat and many of the other neighbors were well into the second event—the Chicken-Soup-Delivery-to-the-Sick. Many thought they could get away with what they had on hand, but one after another carrying tomato, chili beef, and chunky vegetable were turned away at the Pepins' door and disqualified.

"Oh, I am so sorry," said Mrs. Pepin, who was in charge of this event. "If it were up to me, I'd eat it, although honestly, Mrs. Meyer, do you think it's wise to give spicy curry soup to someone who is ailing? Well, yes, I know it's a secret family recipe, but suppose the person has a stomach bug? No, I hadn't heard that spices kill off bugs. Interesting. No, I'm afraid we specified chicken soup quite clearly."

By the time the last person had brought over his soup, Mrs. Pepin was in a dead sweat. "No, I don't think a cow is somewhat like a chicken. Mr. Matthews, you have not seen feathered cows. Yes, I know it's too late to start cooking some fresh. If it were up to me, believe me, you'd all be winners. It is so hard to say no to one's neighbors."

And how right she was, for at that moment Irving and Petunia were playing their parts as magazine, Girl Scout cookie, and raffle ticket sales-children. This was a true test of strength. How many neighbors tried, really tried, to reach for their wallets, but in the end, their strength given out, croaked, "NO! Why *should* I support the soc-cer team? I don't even like soccer!" Yes, they were falling left and right. Thanks to Miss Poopenstat's brief bout with professional coaching, she was able to glide her hand into her purse each and every time, cooing sweet lies about her days as a Girl Scout and even coming up with the correct change. As the pièce de résistance, she gave Irving a tip and ruffled his fluffy hair. "Oooooo," mur-mured the crowd. This was an impressive display of neighborliness.

People were arriving from all over Peony to watch this fascinating contest. Miss Poopenstat was in the lead, closely followed by Mr. Herringbone from down the street, who had his chicken soup all ready and his wallet stocked with dollar bills and blank checks. He also got his Christmas cards off a month early and sent his taxes in on time. It did not make him popular. "What do I care if I am popular so long as I win the Neighbor-Off?" he asked himself.

Mr. Bradshaw, I'm afraid, had lingered to talk to Petunia and Irving when they tried to sell him raffle tickets.

"Mr. Bradshaw," hissed Irving, "I appreciate your friendly loquaciousness, but time is of the essence."

"Old habits die hard," said Mr. Bradshaw. When he saw children, he never could just grab the cookies and shove the money at them.

Now Miss Poopenstat and Mr. Herringbone were on the fourth event, the Return-of-the-Injured-Pet. Miss Poopenstat picked Roy up under her arm like a football and began to run toward Mr. Pepin as if he were a goalpost. "Look out, I'm going out for a pass," she said, throwing Roy across the field to him.

"How does she manage to throw a dog that far?" asked a spectator.

"Practice," said another.

Mr. Herringbone was handicapped by being allergic to cats and was trying to roll Miranda across the lawn with the end of a broom without actually having to come into contact with her.

"Ouch!" shrieked Miranda. "You know, the idea of returning the injured pet is not to inflict as many injuries along the—ouch—way as you—ouch—can!"

"Shut up and roll," said Mr. Herringbone. "We're four seconds behind Poopenstat."

Mr. Bradshaw came over and picked Miranda up. "For heaven's sake, I'll carry her to Mr. Pepin for you," he said to Mr. Herringbone.

"Okay, but I get the ribbon, not you," said Mr. Herringbone.

"Yes, yes," said Mr. Bradshaw, sighing. He handed Miranda to Mr. Pepin and then retrieved Roy from the bushes, where someone imitating Miss Poopenstat but with worse aim had tossed him. Unfortunately, by the time Mr. Bradshaw had received his Injured Pet ribbon, Miss Poopenstat had given her cheery wave to the neighbors on the porch, finishing the last event, and was declared the winner.

"I knew it!" she shrieked. "*I* am the very fine neighbor, and you, Mr. Bradshaw, are an aardvark. Nanny-nanny-boo-boo."

"Drat! Always the bridesmaid, never the bride," said Mr. Herringbone, who came in second and stormed home.

"Madam, I concede your superiority in the contest," said Mr. Bradshaw, doffing his hat and sit-

ting on the Pepins' front porch to drink lemonade with the crowd.

Nelly went up to Miss Poopenstat and gave her a plaque that read VERY FINE NEIGHBOR. Then everyone moved to the Pepins' backyard for a wienie roast and jitterbug contest. Oh, there was no end of contests in that neighborhood that night. And many prizes.

"Stop that!" said Petunia. (She never lets the author have any fun.)

Miss Poopenstat was so tired that she went right to bed. The following week, after nineteen people knocked on her door and asked to borrow a cup of sugar (because, after all, she was the very fine neighbor), she gave up the title in disgust and replaced the old plaque with one that read, I AM AN AARDVARK, SO GO GET YOUR SUGAR SOMEPLACE ELSE and thereafter was not once bothered. Not even by people with ants.

"Ah," said Mr. Pepin as he sat about of a summer's eve on his porch swing with his family gathered around and Mr. Bradshaw swinging from the eaves on a rope swing he had made out of taffy, which he and Petunia were trying out, "sometimes it seems to me that our problems are a blessing in disguise. What do you think, dear family?"

Irving, the sixth-grade genius, replied that blessings were subject to the effect of the Heisenberg Uncertainty Principle like everything else, and it would be fruitless to try to deny it.

Petunia said that if she were a blessing, she would not find it necessary to go around in false nose and glasses or whatever it was Mr. Pepin had in mind.

Roy said that the kibble was getting a bit low.

Miranda asked if he ever thought of anything else.

Mr. Bradshaw told the pets that if they would sit quietly on the porch without squabbling, and try to stick to the main topic of conversation without getting sidetracked by kibble issues, he would let them try his fabulous Bradshaw's exploding mice (fun for both cats and dogs).

And Mrs. Pepin burst into tears.

"Why ever do you suppose she is crying?" asked Mr. Pepin.

"Perhaps her tender heart cannot bear the thought of exploding mice," suggested Petunia.

"Oh, surely even tender hearts rejoice at *that,*" said Miranda.

"Perhaps she has forgotten one of Miss Poopenstat's recipes. She seemed very fond of the broccoli brownies," said Irving.

"Let us hope she has forgotten that," said Petunia.

"Our dear Mrs. Pepin would not cry over such a trifle," said Mr. Pepin. "Why, I have not seen salty droplets grace her rosy cheeks since Mr. Bradshaw discovered we had been trying to pass lemonade squares off as cheese. Now, *there* was an embarrassing situation worth crying over. Perhaps your mother is once again disguising food. Roy, go check the refrigerator."

Roy checked but found all the food was as it should be, although Miranda pointed out that he would hardly know if food was in disguise, since that was the whole point of the disguise.

"There were no pears to trick the eye," said Roy confidently. "As food disguises go, I am onto her."

"Well, that is a relief," said Mr. Pepin, "because

one does not like to feel that one's wife of eighteen years has developed a penchant for disguising one's victuals for sport. And yet I fear that means I have no solution. How shall we ever find out what is troubling her?" Mr. Pepin began to tear up sympathetically.

"Oh dear, oh dear," said Mr. Bradshaw. "I have no advice. Women have eluded me lo these many years. Although she is 'the bonniest babe on the block.' "

"And 'the toe-tappingest tootsie in town,' " agreed Mr. Pepin, and then for a short catastrophic moment the whole family slid into the score of *Babes and Tootsies* until the author reminded them that they were in a children's book and not, as they temporarily and misguidedly believed, a musical.

"This is a problem," said Mr. Pepin, taking a long swig of lemonade—singing and crying are both thirsty work and the combination was positively dehydrating.

"A Pepins' problem," said Irving.

"Well, who else's?" said Mr. Bradshaw a bit

testily. He was enjoying being in a musical and not at all pleased with the author for yanking them off-stage.

Really, I think this chapter had better stop now. They are all becoming extremely disagreeable. Perhaps they have not rested sufficiently after all their neighbor-off excitement. But how are they ever to find out why Mrs. Pepin is crying? We will let them rest now while you, dear readers, help me to solve this, another Pepin (that's children's book Pepin, *not* the musical) problem.

MRS. PEPIN wishes to Be... (well, that would give it away)

Yes, yes, dear readers. Your author almost gave away everything in the title. She would have indeed if a reader from Shaft Ox Corner, Delaware, had not risen up and bitten her in the ankle. Although your author delights in hearing from her readers, she does not wish to feel them. No more teeth. Please. I do not like to say anything against Delawarians, but it is clear to me that their vicious tooth attacks are a bid for attention. I have written a poetic explanation.

I do not wish to denigrate the Delawarian,
But frankly, without their teeth, who is aware of them?

Does anyone know where Delaware is exactly? You see. I know there will be those among you who kindheartedly point out that it's the same with, oh, say, Nevada. But it is not. It is not the same at all.

As you will recall, the problem was that Mrs. Pepin had burst into tears and the Pepins and Mr. Bradshaw did not know how to find out what troubled her.

A reader from Plentywood, Montana (where they don't believe in prepositions), suggested that they find Mrs. Pepin a good hypnotherapist and while she is under begin with such seemingly simple questions as why she keeps her underwear in the chimney, then work up to the matter at hand.

A reader from Funk, Nebraska, which up to now has been, thankfully, a quiet state, murmurs that the author should put Mrs. Pepin on a diet of grain-fed pork until she can no longer stand it. That will teach her. The Funky reader has fallen fearfully far from the mark. No one is trying to

MRS. PEPIN WISHES TO BE . . .

teach anyone anything in this book. But perhaps least of all Mrs. Pepin. Honestly.

Readers from both Rainbow and Hazardville, Connecticut (a state where founding fathers differed in their visions), think that perhaps we should all begin crying and see what happens. Well, perhaps we should. Not.

The true solution comes from a passing Australian. If you pay attention, this often happens. They are frequently hiding in the bushes, just waiting to emerge as dei ex machina. This one strolled casually by murmuring, "Why don't you just ask her?"

Mr. Pepin leaped at the Australian's solution and ran to Mrs. Pepin. "Dear one," he said, as Irving, Petunia, Roy, Miranda, and their very fine neighbor Mr. Bradshaw crept on bended knee to the frighteningly wet Mrs. Pepin, "forgive us for intruding on your histrionics, but do, do, please tell us why you sob."

"Because," wailed Mrs. Pepin in ever-spiraling tones, "I wish to be queen!"

That was a stickler.

"Queen?" asked Miranda.

"Someone forgot to fill my kibble bowl again," said Roy.

"Not king?" said Mr. Bradshaw. "I think you'd make a heck of a king. Just grow a beard. I do urge you, grow a good long one."

"I don't want to grow a beard," sobbed Mrs. Pepin. "I just want to be queen."

"Queen of what?" asked Mr. Pepin, looking worriedly around the yard for something over which Mrs. Pepin could reign.

"I don't know," said Mrs. Pepin, sobbing all the harder.

"A small country perhaps?" inquired Petunia.

"A municipality?" said Irving, ever the practical. "We might be able to scare up one of those."

"Nebraska?" said Miranda. "They could use a queen."

"Kibble?" said Roy.

"Queen of *kibble*?" said Miranda scathingly.

"No, JUST KIBBLE! I am once again OUT OF KIBBLE!" roared Roy. He was a patient dog, but he had his moments, like the rest of us.

"A principality?" asked Mr. Bradshaw.

"No," sobbed Mrs. Pepin. "Then I would have to be prince." To be so misunderstood seemed to further upset her, and Mr. Pepin had to run for her collection of delicate lace handkerchiefs hand-sewn by young tenderhearted girls in some century before television.

"Queen of a state, city, or country?" asked Mr. Pepin. "A small village perhaps?"

"Something . . ." agreed Mrs. Pepin with re-newed waterworks.

"Well then," said Mr. Pepin, "we must find you something in need of ruling."

Mrs. Pepin fell over in gratitude and curled up beneath a pile of handkerchiefs, sobbing with less vigor but no less feeling.

And the Pepins, Roy, Miranda, and their very fine neighbor Mr. Bradshaw went in search of something Mrs. Pepin could be queen of.

"Nothing too small," she called after them in muffled tones.

It is not so easy to find things in need of ruling as you might think. The Pepins searched day and night. All right, they searched day. But they worried about it at night. When they weren't sleeping.

Or playing with exploding mice. Mr. Bradshaw was a constant source of mice in unnatural states.

"Really," said Irving one morning as he attempted to eat the bath brush that Mrs. Pepin had served him for breakfast, "something must be done."

"I agree," said Mr. Pepin, turning over his breakfast of lightly toasted washcloths with a laconic air. Evidently Mrs. Pepin had simply swept up a load of knickknacks from the bathroom for the morning meal. "I get the feeling that Mrs. Pepin is not concentrating."

"Perhaps we should advertise for someone wanting a part-time queen," said Petunia. "You don't suppose she'll want to do this full-time, do you?"

"I don't suppose she can," said Mr. Pepin. "She has Mah-Jongg on Thursdays. And I'm certain she will not want to give up her part-time job at the Domestic Laboratory."

"Ah, peanut butter," said the children.

"The many uses," said Roy and Miranda.

They put their hands and paws to their hearts and then the moment passed.

"Advertising! What a pip of an idea!" said Mr. Bradshaw, who sometimes showed up in his night-cap and slippers for a little morning sustenance. Or, as in the case of this morning, a novelty breakfast. He had been served Q-tips covered in sugar and milk. It hardly improved the flavor. But Mr. Bradshaw, who was often called upon to test his own snack products, had tasted worse.

Irving fetched a pen and paper, and before school and work, he, Mr. Pepin, Petunia, and Mr. Bradshaw drafted a small advertisement for the local paper.

WANTED

Country or similarly grouped peoples
in need of ruling.
Must be able to provide crown jewels
and . . .

Here they paused and sucked on their still rather defective and sticky edible pencils (a gift from Mr. Bradshaw).

"What else do you suppose she requires?" asked Mr. Pepin.

"A penguin or two?" suggested Irving.

"Quite," said Mr. Pepin and wrote:

> *a penguin or two.*
> *Not too small.*

Then, in order to clarify, he added:

> *The country or similarly grouped peoples,*
> *NOT the penguin.*

He sucked on his pencil again and added:

> *But prefer largish penguins as well.*

This out of the way, Mr. Pepin opened a case of Pop-Tarts he kept under the back porch in case of emergencies, and they had a little grovel in the trough before setting out on their busy paths.

The next morning when the ad came out, the telephone began to ring. There was no end of countries and similarly grouped peoples wanting a queen. Unfortunately, few met the Pepins' demand for both crown jewels and penguins. The

Pepins were surprised to find that some countries had the audacity to make their own requirements.

"Can you believe this?" hissed Irving, covering the phone receiver with a cupped palm and addressing the gathered family, who were taking down offers faster than you can say "divine progeniture." "This country wants to know if Mother will behave in any scandalous ways when she takes up her queenship."

"For heaven's sake," said Mr. Pepin. "Assure them she won't."

"You don't understand," said Irving. "They *want* her to. They say it is the whole raison d'être for keeping royalty."

"Is that France calling again?" asked Mr. Pepin impatiently.

Irving nodded.

"Hang up."

In the end they had three viable offers, and of them Mrs. Pepin chose to be queen of Mr. Bilbano's garage because he only lived down the road and it required the least commuting. The coronation was a joyous affair. The crown jewels were taken out of Mr. Bilbano's tool cupboard, and

the penguins all wore very nice necklaces.

"I was wondering what to do with those penguins. They were taking up an awful lot of space in the dining room," said Mr. Bilbano ruminatively as he picked broomstraws out of his teeth. Refreshments had been supplied by Mr. Bradshaw, whose latest snack product was the crumb recycler—a broom which picked up stray cookie crumbs and formed them into newly pressed cookies.

"*Not* a winner," whispered Roy to Miranda, but perhaps he was merely put out because crumb patrol had been one of his just deserts. (The author would like to point out that this little play on words was Roy's. She may wish to entertain, but she has yet to stoop to puns.)

That night, as Mrs. Pepin went to bed, Mr.

Pepin was happy to see her cheeks unblotched and her eyes unbedewed.

"Thank you, my dear," she said, gently kissing Mr. Pepin on his forehead. "Where would I be without you?"

"A lesser sovereign, that's for sure," muttered Mr. Pepin, who had had a rather trying three days, fond though he was of Her Majesty.

"Good night, dear," she said. "Finally we shall all get a little sleep."

Or they would have had Petunia not flown by the window just at that instant.

"Did you tell Petunia she could fly about at this hour?" Mrs. Pepin demanded, turning to Mr. Pepin.

"I?" said Mr. Pepin. "I have been scrupulous about telling the children never to hover. And certainly not to soar."

"Well, hovering and soaring she is!" said Mrs. Pepin in the tone that always drove Mr. Pepin crazy, but before he could answer, Mrs. Pepin threw up the window and poked her head out. "Petunia Pepin!" she called. "It is long past your bedtime. No matter what your father told you, I in-

sist you stop that flying about this instant." But her words were lost on the horizon to which Petunia's parents could see she was swiftly heading.

"There, now you've done it," said Mrs. Pepin. "She's flown the coop."

"*I've* done it?" Mr. Pepin started to screech, and then he remembered that they had both had a very long day, and so he decided to blame Irving. "Irving! Do you know anything about this?"

But unfortunately for Mr. Pepin's purposes, Irving was sound asleep. His large brain needed recharging more than the others', and he often fell asleep for the night as early as dinnertime. Sometimes in the middle of the soup. Not always.

"Well, don't just stand there," barked Mrs. Pepin. (Perhaps she had been queen too long.) "Get her back!"

"Goodness," said Mr. Pepin, scratching his head. "That would seem to be the thing, but there's just one problem."

"What now?" said Mrs. Pepin.

"I don't know how," said Mr. Pepin.

Yikes! Something the Pepins don't know how to do? Surely we can call upon you, dear readers!

A Little Night Flying

Readers have been particularly anxious to help your author with this sticky little problem. After all, when one's loved ones start flying over the horizon, one must take action.

A reader from Bonetrail, North Dakota, suggests that the Pepins move to the Dakotas, where he assures us the horizon is so far away one has plenty of time to retrieve the odds and ends of one's relatives before they completely disappear.

A reader from Ideal, South Dakota (which raises the question, would one rather live in Normal or Ideal?), suggests dog whistles. Your author is making Roy stand outside the house and whistle until he is blue in the face, but Petunia has not reappeared. Apparently, this is not the type of dog whistle this reader means. There seems to be some kind of high-pitched whistle used for calling dogs. Mr. Pepin has gone over to Mr. Bumblebee's house to wake him up. Mr. Bumblebee owns Bumblebee's Miserable Pet Shop. When Mr. Bumblebee hears of the Pepins' problem, he quickly stumbles across

the street to open his shop and sell Mr. Pepin a dog whistle. From now on, it is Bumblebee's for all our pet needs. Of course, his is also the only pet shop in Peony. Mr. Bumblebee tags along while Mr. Pepin tries out the dog whistle. He tells Mr. Pepin that he is pretty sure it works only on dogs. Petunia does not reappear, so perhaps he is right.

A reader from Ten Sleep, Wyoming, suggests a very long fishing line. A reader from Two Egg, Florida, says this is just the type of suggestion one expects from a resident of a landlocked state. Clearly Wyoming knows nothing about fishing. Ten Sleep replies to Two Egg, "Yes? What about fly fishing? Perhaps if there were more than two eggs . . ." And Two Egg says, "Perhaps if more than ten could sleep . . ." And nyah nyah nyah. Honestly, it is at times like this that your author is sorry to have invited you all in to play.

Finally a reader from New Harmony, Utah, suggests that Mr. and Mrs. Pepin, before trekking out to the horizon in search of Petunia, see if she is in her own bed.

"Extraordinary," said Mrs. Pepin, poking her head through Petunia's bedroom doorway. For there lay our little Petunia, safe, sound, and fast asleep.

"I could have sworn I saw her fly over the horizon," said Mr. Pepin, scratching his head.

"For now I think the best thing is to go to bed, dear Mr. Pepin," said Mrs. Pepin, even though they had been on a first-name basis since Friday.

"More will be revealed," agreed Mr. Pepin, and they found their nightcaps and tucked themselves in bed.

The next morning, over crispy waffles, Mr. Pepin said, "Uh, Petunia, dear heart, joy of the morning."

"Angel of the dust bunnies," said Mrs. Pepin.

"Light of my dark dungeon," said Mr. Pepin.

"Chunk of beef among the kibble," joined in Roy.

"Bell of the mouse," said Miranda.

"Overestimated and underworked," said Irving.

"Yes?" said Petunia.

"We had the strangest experience last night," said Mrs. Pepin, "your father and I."

"Your mother and I," said Mr. Pepin in solidarity.

"We thought, heh heh heh." Mrs. Pepin chortled apologetically to keep Petunia from dwelling on plans to have her and Mr. Pepin committed at the earliest opportunity. "We thought we saw you fly past the window."

"There, it's out," said Mr. Pepin, crossing his arms over his chest.

"Excellent!" said Petunia, hardly looking up from her waffles.

"Not excellent at all," disagreed Mrs. Pepin mildly. "Your father and I do not wish to see things fly past our window that (A) do not fly and (B) are actually in bed at the time we see them flying."

"How far did I go?" asked Petunia, which to Mrs. Pepin's way of thinking rather missed the point.

"Right past the horizon; you could certainly soar, I'll give you that," said Mr. Pepin, "even though, as it turns out, you didn't."

"Perfect. Exactly as I had hoped. I shall get an A for sure," said Petunia.

"Whatever are you babbling about?" asked Mrs. Pepin, thinking that perhaps it would be Petunia who would be committed. Heh heh heh heh.

"You did see me fly," said Petunia. "And yet you did not."

"Come again?" said Mrs. Pepin.

"I seemed to disappear across the horizon and yet I was in bed," said Petunia.

"So far we have covered this ground," said Mr. Pepin.

"Let the girl speak," said Mrs. Pepin, thinking there would be plenty of time to ignore her when she was in the booby hatch.

"I did not say I flew. I said you saw me fly," said Petunia.

"Oh dear," said Mrs. Pepin. "It's like those horrible Sphinx-type riddles."

Fortunately, Irving the sixth-grade genius's brain was fueled by sixteen waffles and half a bottle of syrup, and he supplied the obvious answer. "Of course," he said. "It was all done with mirrors. A science project?" Because it was his long-suffering experience that when things start to fly around the house or foam, it is usually a science project.

"Exactly," said Petunia. "You see, my teacher asked each of us to come up with an example of optical illusion. I quickly checked out twenty-nine books from the library about magicians and their tricks, for who is more optically illuded than they? To fly seemed to be the thing. Mirrors. Remarkable. Now I must catch the school bus."

The children dashed off to get their bus, and Mr. Pepin drove Mrs. Pepin to the train station, to take their different trains to work.

"It is remarkable what can be done with mirrors, isn't it?" said Mr. Pepin as he parked the car.

"And," said Mrs. Pepin, "what can be done without them."

They nodded happily. It is well to have such things settled before the 8:05 pulls in. Mrs. Pepin saw Mr. Bradshaw, blew Mr. Pepin a kiss, and ran off to join their very fine neighbor. Mrs. Pepin and Mr. Bradshaw took the same train to work, and Mrs. Pepin was anxious to tell Mr. Bradshaw what she and Mr. Pepin had concluded about mirrors, but she found him singularly preoccupied.

"Mr. Bradshaw," she said when he had twice failed to comment on the remarkableness of mirrors, "you are singularly preoccupied."

"Usually with anchovies," said Mr. Bradshaw,

getting off at his station, "and a light Chardonnay."

"Well, really," said Mrs. Pepin, "I don't like the sound of that."

That evening after dinner, and after Mrs. Pepin had spent her evening hour in Mr. Bilbano's garage reigning, as the family slowly filed into the living room to bask in the firelight and eat dry corn twinklies, Mrs. Pepin brought up the strange preoccupation of their very fine neighbor Mr. Bradshaw.

"Hardly seemed to know I was there," said Mrs. Pepin.

"I fear I have had the same experience with him lately," said Mr. Pepin. "He appeared to be leaving his house for work wearing his house slippers. When I pointed this out to him, he muttered, 'That won't do. What would she think?' and trotted back in to change. He came back wearing ice skates, but I hardly felt like commenting on that."

"A man can stand only so much criticism," agreed Mrs. Pepin. "Although I'm sure you did not mean to be critical, dear."

"Pointing out improper footwear has always

been a sign of caring, where I come from," agreed Mr. Pepin. "And yet it wasn't that he was offended but rather, as in your experience, that he didn't seem to know I was there at all."

"Perhaps he knew but did not care," said Roy sourly, having been twice refused what he deemed to be his fair share of corn twinklies.

"He invited me over to help him with his snack product experiments. We were to test some chocolate-flavored motor oil," said Irving, "but I fear he is not up to his old inventing high standards."

"It wasn't delicious?" asked Mrs. Pepin.

"It was not," said Irving. "And when I pointed this out to him—that it tasted like it still had motor oil in it—he said, 'I said chocolate-*flavored* motor oil. Of course it must taste like chocolate. But it must also contain motor oil. That's what makes it authentic. That's what gives it its zip!' "

"I do not like the idea of your drinking motor oil," said Mrs. Pepin.

"I did not think you would, and when I pointed this out to him, he said, 'Do you think all women feel the same?' " said Irving. "I didn't know what he meant and didn't ask and at any rate was in a hurry to get home and wash the remaining dregs of motor oil out of my mouth."

"I have been worried about dear Mr. Bradshaw myself," said Petunia. "Yesterday I sat on the porch and he drifted by saying, 'Gertrude? Melanie? Alice? Kate? Hermione? Alicia? Maud?' "

"Hmmm," said Mrs. Pepin. "Something does seem to be on his mind, and I think we now have some clues."

"Some clues?" said Mr. Pepin. "We are not in a detective story."

(Your author would like to point out that they are in whatever she thinks they are in, so there.)

"Yes, some clues to what is so preoccupying our good friend and very fine neighbor Mr. Bradshaw," said Mrs. Pepin.

"It's quite a problem," said Mr. Pepin.

Indeed it was. Which is why I would prevail upon you, dear readers, to help us solve this, another Pepin problem. Not a detective story. Not a musical. I *could* put in a little earnest sad longing and change it into an adult novel. (Oh no, I can feel my editor giving me warning squints. All right, all right.)

Mr. Bradshaw Steps Out

Readers from all over the nation are thought-projecting their solutions until your dear author's head is swimming. Some of you could turn down your rock 'n' roll in the background. If you'd care to play some gentle songs about hard times coming again no more and other uplifting tunes, I would not object. Also if you'd care to send me a fruitcake.

A reader from Last Chance, Colorado (a nervous place to live), says that Mr. Bradshaw is probably reading a good book. That whenever she reads a good book, it is all she can think about for days.

A book like *The Pepins and Their Problems,* asks your author? There is no answer. Some of our readers are flibbertigibbets.

A reader from Captain Cook, Hawaii, says perhaps Mr. Bradshaw has sunstroke. People in Hawaii are always walking along sunstruck. Your author suggests they might just get out of the sun. There, she has solved this, another reader problem. HAHAHA.

A reader from Sedro-Woolley, Washington, and a reader from Washington, D.C. (where they are always whining about not being included in this type of thing—sssh), are saying at the same time that perhaps Mr. Bradshaw is planning on taking over the world. That tends to be time-consuming unless one has a *really* good plan.

A reader from Duckwater, Nevada, said he thought so, too, and perhaps Mr. Bradshaw had joined forces with the aliens. Your author refers you to the first chapter and her opinion on these alien goings-on.

Mrs. Pepin was really quite worried about Mr. Bradshaw. She said he had been a very fine neighbor all these years, and suppose he was in the grips of something big, and she did not mean extra-terrestrially.

"Yes," said Petunia, "and suppose he moves."

"And a new family moves in," said Irving. "A family that lives on marshmallow biscuit sandwiches."

"Property values will go down," said Mr. Pepin.

"We must do something," said Petunia.

"How could we let things go this far unresolved?" asked Irving.

They all ran to the window to see if the FOR SALE sign had been posted yet, but it had not.

"Whew," said Mr. Pepin. "A lucky break."

"We must have Mr. Bradshaw for dinner," said Mrs. Pepin. "We must have him for dinner and speak to him. Quite sharply if necessary."

"Yes, get him to snap out of it," agreed Petunia.

"Whatever it is," said Mr. Pepin.

"I will make chicken," said Mrs. Pepin thoughtfully. "Everyone likes chicken."

And so it was that Mr. Bradshaw assumed his regular place at the old Pepin family board and they plied him with chicken and potatoes and corn and beans and many healthy things and no biscuits or marshmallows because after that morning's conversation Mrs. Pepin had developed an unnatural fear of them.

"And now," said Mr. Pepin as Mrs. Pepin sliced the pie, "my dear friend and neighbor, you must tell us what is up."

"Hmmm, what's that?" asked Mr. Bradshaw. He had been saying "Hmmm, what's that?" whenever addressed during dinner. The rest of the time he said nothing but hummed "It Had to Be You."

"You seem preoccupied," said Mrs. Pepin, passing him a piece of pie and wringing her hands. "It's peach, your favorite," she added quaveringly.

"Where will you go? That's what I want to know," said Petunia, putting her head down on the tablecloth, giving way to her emotions, and blowing her nose on her napkin.

"What's that?" said Mr. Bradshaw with even greater puzzlement but hoping Mrs. Pepin washed the napkins after every meal.

"Think, man! Think!" ordered Mr. Pepin. "Come to your senses! You can't move to California or Hawaii."

"Sunstroke," said Mrs. Pepin reasonably.

"And where does that leave you?" asked Mr. Pepin.

"I beg your pardon," said Mr. Bradshaw, taking a big bite of pie. For someone so preoccupied he was very focused on his pie. "But am I moving?"

"Yes," sobbed Petunia.

"Why?" asked Mr. Bradshaw in alarm, for this was the first he had heard of it.

"Because you're in the grips of something big," said Irving.

"True enough. Well said," said Mr. Bradshaw. "*La belle femme* in the striped dress."

"What's a *belle femme*?" asked Petunia.

"Beautiful woman," said Irving, who was such a sixth-grade genius that he could translate languages even when he didn't speak them.

"Oh, forevermore," said Mrs. Pepin, so startled she sat down without handing out any more pie and began to pick distractedly at the crust until Miranda moved it gently out of her reach. "For-ever-more, Mr. Bradshaw! *You're in love!*"

"Yes," said Mr. Bradshaw, getting out a handkerchief and wiping his dewy brow. "I am indeed."

"Come, then, man," said Mr. Pepin. "Out with it. Who is it? Let us invite her for dinner."

"Does she like chicken?" asked Mrs. Pepin thoughtfully.

"I do not know, for I fear I have not worked up the courage to speak to her yet. I stroll by her corner each day. I do not know her name, but I think of her always as the lovely Rebecca."

"Her corner?" asked Mr. Pepin with some concern.

"She stands outside Harper's barbershop. A tall, lovely, lithe, poetic figure of a woman, her gentle long locks waving in the breeze. I am smitten. Quite smitten. I am smitten with a capital 'S.' "

"Good for you," said Mr. Pepin, losing interest. "Now let us finish our pie. It is getting late, and soon the seven o'clock news will be on." Mr. Pepin, like many of the less gentle sex, had a short attention span when it came to romance. Mr. Pepin's was so short that Mrs. Pepin said it was amazing it had endured long enough to get the ring upon her finger. They loved each other, understand, but Mr. Pepin's idea of a romantic evening out was a good steak dinner followed by a hockey game.

"Whatever shall I do?" asked Mr. Bradshaw.

"Perhaps Mr. Pepin is not the best person to ask," said Mrs. Pepin.

"You must speak to this vision with the long, waving locks," said Petunia. "To see if her conversation lives up to her hair."

"Invite her out for a good steak dinner, that's my advice," said Mr. Pepin.

"And a hockey game," said Irving, who had had *the talk* with his father about such things.

"I cannot, I cannot speak to her," said Mr. Bradshaw pleadingly. "She is too lovely and fair. You must go speak to her for me."

"Who?" asked Mrs. Pepin. "Me?"

"Whoever," said Mr. Bradshaw. "And here, give her this." He whipped a rose out of his breast pocket. It had been there all week and was a bit wilted. Mr. Bradshaw's skin was positively awash with thorn holes. Mrs. Pepin took the rose from him and sniffed it. It seemed to have lost its roselike smell.

"Are you sure this is what you want to give her?" asked Mrs. Pepin.

"You must tell her that I think of her by day and dream of her by night," said Mr. Bradshaw.

It was here that Mr. Pepin and Irving were overcome with a strong desire to leave the room. Perhaps even to join an African safari made up only of manly men in mufti. "I beg of you to say no such thing," said Mr. Pepin.

"Oh," said Mr. Bradshaw in alarm. "But what, pray, should I say to a woman? This is my first romance."

"Say 'Pass the steak sauce!' " suggested Mr. Pepin.

"And 'He shoots! He scores!' " added Irving.

"I think you're doing just fine on your own," said Mrs. Pepin reassuringly to Mr. Bradshaw. "After all, Mr. Pepin, 'Pass the steak sauce' and 'He shoots, he scores' cannot be said by everyone as *you* say it. Now, Mr. Bradshaw, I shall trot out first thing tomorrow if you tell me what time this mystery woman stands in front of the barbershop."

"She seems to be there at all times, the lovely Rebecca. It's quite fortuitous," said Mr. Bradshaw. "Why, whenever I go by the barbershop, taking care to stay on the other side of the street so as not to overwhelm her with my ardent feelings, she is there."

"Perhaps she lies in wait for you," said Petunia. "Perhaps you have caught *her* eye as well."

"Or perhaps she is psychically in tune with you and knows when you approach and positions herself thusly," suggested Mrs. Pepin. She and Petunia just loved this kind of speculation. Also she was very fond of the word "thusly."

"Perhaps she has a job hawking razors," said Mr. Pepin. "Well, if you'll excuse me, the news is on."

"Yes, you must excuse us," said Irving, leaping up and making a dash for it.

"Don't you worry," said Mrs. Pepin, leading Mr. Bradshaw gently to the door. "I will give her your rose and I will ask her her real name because you cannot keep calling her the lovely Rebecca forever."

"Unless, of course, it happens to be her name, after all," said Petunia.

"And I shall ask her to dinner," said Mrs. Pepin.

"You are a saint," said Mr. Bradshaw gratefully.

"Oh no, not I," murmured Mrs. Pepin.

"Yes, a great saint," said Mr. Bradshaw.

"Well, perhaps one of the lesser ones," demurred Mrs. Pepin.

The next day when Petunia got home from school, she and Mrs. Pepin put on their best dresses and their going-to-check-out-someone's-paramour shoes. They donned their good coats and hats, but decided against the gloves in case Mr. Bradshaw's object of affection was of a more casual biker-chick persuasion, and set off for Main Street and the barbershop.

"This is quite exciting. I feel just like the Nurse in *Romeo and Juliet*," said Mrs. Pepin.

"I feel the same," said Petunia, who had not read *Romeo and Juliet* but always agreed with Mrs. Pepin because she had not yet reached the teenage years. "Do you think we should speak to her or give her the rose first?"

"Speak, surely," said Mrs. Pepin. "We do not want her to think we are selling roses."

"I cannot wait to meet her. I never thought of

Mr. Bradshaw as anything but a very fine neighbor and a resolute bachelor."

"Oh, a wedding would be so lovely. We could have it in the backyard," said Mrs. Pepin.

"Nelly would like that. She loves weddings," said Petunia as they approached the barbershop. And there they stopped short, for there was no woman. None at all. There was, however, a brand-new red-and-white-striped barber pole with a brown wind sock attached to the top, waving gently in the breeze.

Petunia and Mrs. Pepin spent a good three minutes staring at it with their mouths open, neither wanting to be the one to give voice to such traitorous thoughts.

"You don't suppose he's in love with a barber pole?" asked Petunia finally.

"They say there is no accounting for taste when it comes to love," said Mrs. Pepin. "I have had college roommates who have done worse."

"She has excellent posture," said Petunia.

"And I'm sure she's very quiet," said Mrs. Pepin thoughtfully. "But I'm rethinking the chicken."

She and Petunia shook their heads very slowly.

Well, it is so seldom one likes both members of a couple. Mrs. Pepin knew one had to make allowances.

"I had at least hoped he would pick someone animate," said Mrs. Pepin, vowing that this was the last discouraging remark she would utter on the subject.

"I think she must have lured him unfairly," said Petunia.

"With her stripes!" agreed Mrs. Pepin.

"No! No!" said Petunia. "I just cannot believe Mr. Bradshaw, our very fine neighbor, would pick a barber pole as a potential spouse."

"They have yet to marry! There is still time!" said Mrs. Pepin, rallying.

"No, no, I mean, there must be some mistake. How *could* Mr. Bradshaw have chosen a barber pole to fall in love with? When he isn't exploding mice, he is quite in his right mind."

"I don't know. I simply don't know," said Mrs. Pepin.

Do you, dear reader?

THE Pepins' PLAN

Naturally, readers from all over have been trying to figure out how Mr. Bradshaw could have fallen in love with a barber pole, attractive though such poles are. A reader from Atomic City, Idaho, says that it could happen to anyone. His own Aunt Celia once fell in love with a bottle of salad dressing and refused to get rid of it even though it was two years past the pull date.

A reader in Coosawhatchie, South Carolina, says that perhaps Mr. Bradshaw has been falling in love with twigs since he was a lad and is working his way up. These things are relative. These things are not relative, says your author. No one wants a barber pole for a relative. The reader from Coosawhatchie says that is not what he means, but your author doesn't really care. Please be quiet, all of you; I am trying to write.

"The problem is a sticky one, that is for sure," said Mr. Pepin, wiping his fingers on his napkin as they all sat about the family board, having just finished pieces of Mrs. Pepin's excellent treacle pudding. Mrs. Pepin had taken to reading Victorian melodramas, in which a treacle pudding inevitably surfaces, and she wanted to experience one firsthand. "How *do* you get treacle pudding off your fingers in a genteel manner?"

"You mean without licking them, I presume?" said Petunia.

"Quite," said Mr. Pepin. He had taken to using British locutions to indulge Mrs. Pepin.

"The problem really is how to ask Mr. Bradshaw why he has fallen in love with a barber pole," said Mrs. Pepin, who had gotten them a finger bowl each for their treacly fingers.

"Ah yes," said Mr. Pepin, "that too."

"It is a question I have long pondered," said

Mrs. Pepin, sitting back in her chair and passing the walnuts and port. "If one's dearest friend should happen to fall in love with a barber pole, should one tell him?"

"Presumably he already knows," said Petunia.

"Not necessarily," said Irving. "There could be extenuating circumstances."

"What kinds of circumstances could cause one to fall in love with a barber pole without knowing about it?" asked Petunia.

"Or," said Mr. Pepin, who was very wise as well as hopped up on all that treacle, "what kinds of circumstances would cause one to fall in love with a barber pole without realizing it *was* a barber pole?"

"Ah," said the rest of the Pepins.

In case you were wondering where Miranda and Roy have been through all this, they were at a meeting of the kennel club.

"As I see it," said Mr. Pepin, "the thing to do is follow him."

"Yes," said Irving, who thought things might finally be picking up. All this love talk was intensely boring, but on the horizon he glimpsed the possibility of sneaking around in trench coats and fedoras. Now, that was more like it. "We should dig some of the hats out of the closet that we used to decorate the Long-Lost Pepin. Disguised in those and perhaps trench coats, we could track him without his noticing."

The Pepins raced around the house and found all the necessary hats and overcoats, and the next Saturday morning at the crack of dawn they hid in Mr. Bradshaw's bushes, waiting for him to rise.

"Remember," said Mrs. Pepin, who had given everyone a pencil and notebook, "write down any suspicious behavior. We do not as yet know what will be important."

"We need more clues," agreed Petunia.

"Clues are the essence of the hunt," said Mr. Pepin. He was looking quite dapper, with a meerschaum pipe hanging out of his mouth. It was a bubble pipe, and large soapy bubbles drifted lazily across Mr. Bradshaw's lawn.

"Oh dear," said Mrs. Pepin, "I do hope that doesn't attract too much attention."

"If anyone appears to be studying me too closely, I will say, 'I say now, nothing like a bubble pipe after your morning treacle pudding.' "

"Ah," said Mrs. Pepin, catching his drift immediately, "and they will mistake you for an English gentleman and fail to look more closely."

"Exactly," said Mr. Pepin happily.

"Ssssh," said Irving, "here he comes."

Mr. Bradshaw came out on the front porch to fetch his morning paper. Unfortunately, Roy was so used to being accommodating that he ran barking onto the porch and brought the paper to Mr. Bradshaw before he could bend down and retrieve it himself.

"My goodness, Roy," said Mr. Bradshaw, peering about in surprise. "What are you doing out and about at this hour by yourself? Is Mr. Pepin with you? Or perhaps Irving is taking you for an early morning walk?" Mr. Bradshaw looked straight into the bushes at the Pepins, but they must have been very well disguised because he did not even seem to see them. "Hmm, and is that a bubble stuck to your ear?" Mr. Bradshaw leaned down and touched it. "Odd. Were you taking a bath? Strange sort of morning. Dogs. Bubbles on ears," Mr. Bradshaw murmured to himself, not seeming to notice that his entire lawn was now full of bubbles. He headed

back inside, walking first into the screen door.

"He doesn't seem to be noticing much," said Petunia, writing furiously in her notebook.

"No, he does not," said Mrs. Pepin, writing as well. "But that would certainly coincide with his being in love, don't you think? I believe gentlemen in such circumstances frequently drift about in a fog."

148

"We must keep an open mind," said Mr. Pepin.

"And take notes," said Petunia, who really liked her little notebook. She liked it so much she was taking notes about the rest of the family as well. "Irving has some spinach stuck to the tip of his nose," she wrote. "Why spinach? We did not have spinach for dinner last night. Or breakfast. Miranda is scratching. Did she take her flea pill this month? Or does she pretend to take her pills and hide them in Roy's kibble? Why did we not know that there was a meershaum bubble pipe in the house until last night? What else has Father been hiding? Why can Mother never remember that the lightbulbs in the house are no longer edible?"

Petunia scribbled away for some time, and while she did, the rest of the Pepins were becoming restive.

"I say," said Mr. Pepin, who had begun to believe he *was* an Englishman. "Getting a bit tedious, not to mention damp and dewy, here under this bush."

"Would you like to move to the mulberry bushes perhaps?" asked Mrs. Pepin.

"What are we going to do if Mr. Bradshaw never leaves his house?" asked Irving. "How will we follow him if he refuses to lead?"

(Yes, yes, I know, were we further along in the story, this might be another Pepin problem, but we are only halfway through the chapter.)

"We must roust him!" said Mrs. Pepin, jumping to her feet enthusiastically. She had always wanted to roust someone even though she had no clear idea what it meant.

"How very barbaric," said Miranda. "Besides which, we have no matches."

"ROUST, not roast, you ninny!" said Roy. He was going about the lawn trying to get another bubble to stick to his ear. He liked the look.

"How do you propose we do that?" asked Irving. "We are all in disguise."

"It is very simple," said Petunia. "We knock on his door and ask him if he can't please go somewhere so that we can follow him."

"Yes," said Mr. Pepin. "By George, I think she's got it!"

The only two Englishmen that Mr. Pepin knew

were Sherlock Holmes and Henry Higgins. He was doing his best to become an amalgamation of the two.

All of the Pepins and Roy and Miranda crept around to Mr. Bradshaw's back door, which opened on his kitchen. He was sitting at his kitchen table eating corn twinklies and reading his paper.

"I say," said Mr. Pepin, tapping lightly on the window. "What's for a spot of a walk, eh?"

Mr. Bradshaw looked up. He was having a difficult time understanding Mr. Pepin, as would an Englishman. Mr. Pepin had developed his own dialect known to no particular country, but it seemed to please him, and that, after all, is the important thing.

"Spot spot, chip chop, fish and chips, take a whirl, eh?" Mr. Pepin went on.

"Who are you and what are you doing dressed in silly hats at my kitchen window?" asked Mr. Bradshaw.

"We were hoping you would take a walk. Good sir." Irving added the "good sir" on second thought,

hoping that perhaps Mr. Bradshaw would think they were all English. Somehow four Englishmen seemed more plausible than one.

"Take a walk?" said Mr. Bradshaw. "But I'm eating my corn twinklies."

"It's a lovely day to get some air," said Mrs. Pepin hopefully.

"Well," said Mr. Bradshaw, considering, "I *was* just thinking that perhaps sometime today I would stroll by the barbershop."

"There you have it, that's the ticket, the very swill," said Mr. Pepin.

"But I hadn't planned on being followed by a bunch of Englishmen," said Mr. Bradshaw.

"Life's funny that way," agreed Mr. Pepin.

"Well, do come in and have some corn twinklies while I get dressed," said Mr. Bradshaw, who was not called the very fine neighbor for nothing.

The Pepins were delighted to proceed into Mr. Bradshaw's kitchen and devour his whole box of corn twinklies.

"We are doing all of this for his own good," Mr. Pepin reminded them through a mouthful of milk. "Perhaps we are eating his corn twinklies under false pretenses, but I don't think anyone could blame us."

The walk behind Mr. Bradshaw proved very edifying. He said good morning to a traffic light, commented to a passing neighbor who happened to have a caterpillar under his nose that he had grown a very fine mustache, came very close three times to stepping directly on Miranda, and bowed with courtly charm and said, "Good morning to you, ma'am," to the milkman.

"You know," said Mrs. Pepin, thoughtfully writing all this down, "light is beginning to dawn."

"Ah, light dawning," said Irving.

"Right, counterpanes and bank holidays, tuckshops and all that," said Mr. Pepin, who was clearly coming to the end of his British vocabulary.

"Mr. Bradshaw," said Mrs. Pepin, ripping off her disguise, "follow me to Dr. Dan's office."

"I beg your pardon, I thought *you* were supposed to be following *me*," said Mr. Bradshaw politely.

"Yes, I have, and very educational it has been. Mr. Bradshaw, you need GLASSES!" said Mrs. Pepin.

"AH!" said all the Pepins. They escorted Mr. Bradshaw to Dr. Dan's, where he was that very morning outfitted with a stunning pair of spectacles. The Pepins then took him home, where he sat on their front porch and narrated the morning.

"Here comes a car! Look, a squirrel! By the great horned spoon, did you know all those bushes had leaves? Another squirrel! By golly, another car!" etc., etc., etc. It became extremely tedious, but the Pepins were forbearing people.

"Yes," said Petunia to Mrs. Pepin as they fixed

a luncheon tray in the kitchen to take to the porch. They could see they were not going to get Mr. Bradshaw off that porch. "It's delightful that his sight is restored, but it doesn't solve the real problem, which is what are we to do when he discovers that he is in love with a barber pole?"

"Tut, tut," said Mrs. Pepin, "I think we will do what we would do, if, say, he had found himself in love with a frying pan. We will accept her into the family with open arms."

But as it turned out, the Pepins did not have to act on this sentiment because the very next day Mr. Bradshaw announced that his romance was unrequited. Having discovered his love was a barber pole, he had nonetheless approached her as a gentleman should, making allowances for the fact she neither could hear him nor was sentient, and had declared himself. He feared, however, he had been refused. Although it was difficult under the circumstances to tell.

"However, good fortune shines on me, for no sooner had my heart recovered from this blow than it began to beat anew. At the very moment of rejection, a vision exited the barbershop."

"Are we talking genuine human this time?" asked Irving rather rudely.

"A Miss Cornelia Howndogger. She is the new manicurist at the barbershop. My heart beats again, clip clop, clip clop."

"His heart beats clip clop?" asked Petunia. "Could this be the trouble?"

"Sssh," said Mrs. Pepin. "Let us just be thankful that when we ask her to dinner we will not have to carry plates out to the sidewalk."

"And she has very kindly agreed to accompany me to a concert tonight. She has a great quantity of curly blond hair, and she speaks."

"A little conversation is always nice," agreed Mrs. Pepin.

And so the Pepins breathed a sigh of relief and went about their business. Mr. Bradshaw took a long walk to see what else he had been missing with his nearsighted eyes. Roy and Miranda went to the movies, where they sat throwing jujubes at the screen during the yucky love parts—they'd had quite enough of that lately—until management threw them out. It wasn't until two weeks had passed that Mr. Bradshaw announced that he would like to have the Pepins meet Miss Howndog-ger. Mrs. Pepin immediately invited them for Sunday dinner, and when she told the family they said, "Dinner? Together?" Because truly for the past two weeks they seemed to have forgotten this ritual. Come to think of it, they seemed to have been eating with their hands for two weeks. "What will we do for cutlery?"

"How these things creep up on you," said Mrs. Pepin in dismay. She went to the cutlery drawer and there was not a spoon or knife there. Nor in the dishwasher. "Where can our eating implements be?"

I hope, dear reader, you are not so worn out by the last true tale of love lost and found that you cannot help solve this, another Pepin problem.

THE PEPINS BEHAVE LIKE RELICS OF A Lesser Civilization

Readers everywhere have been thought-projecting their solutions. It turns out that trying to find eating utensils is not at all an uncommon problem in North American households. In fact, take-out has become so prevalent that finding the kitchen is sometimes the issue. But it was a new experience for the Pepins, who always felt that no matter what happened during the day, the family together around the table at night poured reassuring oil upon the waters. However, your author can see the state of affairs we have gotten ourselves into when she notes the readers' responses.

A reader from Rhode Island says that there are plenty of plastic utensils in the little bins by the food court. Your author declines even to comment on this. No, she will comment: this is not a solution, she suggests, this is a disaster. No wonder, she says, that Rhode Island is full of places called Great Swamp, Worden Pond, or, her personal favorite, Yawgoo Pond. In fact, this reader happens to be from Yawgoo Pond, where take-out isn't an option but a necessity. But your author mustn't editorialize.

A reader from West Virginia, state of Ikes Fork, Slaty Fork, Northfork, Sand Fork, Glen Fork, and, your author's personal favorite, Forks of Cacapon, says that there in West Virginia they revere their eating utensils, which your author finds surprising because it's also the state of Lost River, Lost Creek, and Lost City. A state that hangs on to its eating utensils but loses its cities is not necessarily to be trusted.

The true solution came from a reader in Mashpee, Massachusetts, who says that perhaps if the Pepins would eat an occasional meal together so that someone could keep track of the washing up, there would not be this problem.

"Oh dear," said Mrs. Pepin. "How long has it been since we have had a true family dinner?" Mrs. Pepin had encouraged them all to get involved in their community at the same time, unfortunately, that Mr. Pepin had encouraged them to make good use of their coming summertime. School would be out soon, he said, and they should begin registering immediately for classes and activities so as not to miss the summer fun boat. An involved Pepin is, after all, a happy Pepin.

So they kept adding activities several at a time, and now that school was out, they were suddenly all up to their ears with Scouts and gymnastics, bowling leagues, union meetings, knitting bees, hockey, soccer, ballet, show jumping, skittles, bridge clubs, library guilds, Habitat for Humanity, improv, choir, basketball, and semiprofessional wrestling. And that was just Monday. For two weeks they continued to pile on exciting new ventures, knowing the long empty days of summer were upon them, until it became increasingly difficult to have a meal together. The Pepins, I'm afraid, had become as relics of a lesser civilization. Slowly, frozen chicken strip by frozen chicken strip, they had wandered down that slippery slope, with Mrs. Pepin doing the work of a short-order cook at first, and finally people rummaging in peanut butter jars and granola bar boxes.

"We are slobs," wept Mrs. Pepin.

"But extremely well-rounded ones," said Mr. Pepin, doing a backflip off the banister, for it was he who had taken up gymnastics.

"What, after all, is the good of civilization if its members merely grab at saber-toothed tiger bones, gnawing them in passing?" demanded Mrs. Pepin, who, once wound up, could go on for quite a while in this vein.

"It wasn't saber-toothed tiger, it was Chinese take-out mostly," said Petunia. "And things micro-wavable."

"It is fortunate that Mr. Bradshaw and Miss Howndogger will be dining with us on Sunday. It will get us back on track," insisted Mrs. Pepin.

But Sunday morning dawned and the whirl-wind was still going strong. Those who did not have meetings of one kind or another had home-work and practice. And worse, thought Mrs. Pepin, the forks were still missing. Mrs. Pepin knew she had to do something drastic. So she stood on her roof and rang a bell. She did not know why she stood on the roof. Perhaps it was nostalgia for the beginning of their problems, when the house was a haven for the family and not merely a terminal between activities. Perhaps she merely liked standing on rooftops. Who can say?

However, a Pepin, when he or she hears a rooftop bell, heeds the call. Within ten minutes all Pepins were on the roof, even Roy and Miranda. The neighbor from down the street was trotting over with his pikestaff, but the Pepins called down that this time they had a ladder, and he returned home disappointed.

"You probably wonder why I have summoned you here," said Mrs. Pepin. "I have summoned you here for a family meeting."

"It seems cruel to have a meeting someplace where Nelly cannot join us," interrupted Petunia.

They looked down. Indeed, Nelly was standing under the gutter looking up at them with betrayed eyes. The rest of the morning was spent in trying to get Nelly onto the roof. Mr. Pepin finally signaled to Mr. Bradshaw, who was on the porch, and by a series of intricate flag-waving movements and Morse code they were able to communicate that they wished Mr. Bradshaw to invent a way to get

Nelly onto the roof. He did so with a series of small rockets. Nelly did not enjoy the ride, but once on the roof, she said the view was swell. Unfortunately, her weight was too much for the roof to bear, and she fell through into the Pepins' bathtub. She was not hurt, but it didn't do the porcelain any good.

"Nelly dear, do stay put, and we'll join you down there for our meeting," said Mrs. Pepin. They all jumped down to the bathroom. "Now, the reason I have called you all together—"

"Ouch," said Nelly.

"The reason—" Mrs. Pepin began again, thinking Nelly was suffering from a charley horse.

"Ouch, ouch, darn it," said Nelly.

"Nelly, what is it?" asked Mrs. Pepin. She was feeling, rather uncharitably, that Nelly *might* suffer silently until she was done explaining.

"I seem to have something caught in my hoof," said Nelly.

"Well, if it can just wait five minutes, dear, what I wanted to say to the family is that we are having something of a crisis. It is now noontime. I have in-

165

vited our guests for a three o'clock family dinner. So far we have no dinner and we have no eating utensils and, frankly, up until quite recently and our roof reunion, we seemed to have no family."

"Let us not indulge in hyperbole," said Nelly.

"How I do like a little hyperbolosity around midday," said Mr. Pepin.

"We also have a hole in our roof," said Irving.

"I am becoming very late for tap dancing," said Petunia.

"I did not know you were taking tap-dancing lessons," said Mrs. Pepin. "Although, these days, who can keep track?"

"I'm not," said Petunia, "but I always try to tap-dance around the house at eleven o'clock Sunday morning."

"And why is that?" asked Mr. Pepin.

"It's the only time slot available. And a one tappy tappy and a two tappy tappy," said Petunia.

"Listen, will someone *please* look at my foot!" begged Nelly.

"Yes, of course," said Petunia, tapping over to her. She picked up Nelly's hoof. "Oh my!"

"Oh my what?" asked Nelly.

"You seem to have a fork stuck in it," said Petunia, gently pulling out the fork and holding it up for all to see.

"A fork?" said Mrs. Pepin.

"How extraordinary," said Mr. Pepin. "I myself am in the habit of pulling spoons out of my feet."

"Perhaps not as extraordinary as you think," said Irving. "I seem to remember eating a small single-serving take-out quiche while taking a bath."

"AHA!" said Mrs. Pepin. "A clue!"

"A small single-serving take-out quiche? Where will it lead us?" pondered Mr. Pepin.

"No, no, it is the fork that is the clue," said Mrs. Pepin. "Is this what has become of the cutlery? Abandoned piecemeal after lonely meals in odd places?"

"Should we get our trench coats?" asked Irving hopefully.

"No time," said Mrs. Pepin. "We know what we must do."

"We must walk around the house avoiding stepping on forks," said Mr. Pepin.

"Or, in your case, spoons," said Petunia.

"No, no," said Mrs. Pepin frantically. Did no one understand? Had her family truly deserted her, psychically if not physically? "We must find all the cutlery scattered about the house. Can't you see what has happened? We have been eating over sinks, in bathtubs, in beds, under beds, on porches, wherever and whenever, for two weeks and throwing the cutlery down absentmindedly. We need to retrieve it all, wash it, set the table, cook a dinner, and then we can greet our guests like the normal family that we are."

"Will someone please help me out of this bathtub?" implored Nelly.

All tried and failed. It was a soaker tub with very high, slippery curved sides, and they could get no purchase on Nelly.

"Nelly, you need handles," said Irving irritably.

"Like a mattress," agreed Petunia.

"This will not do," said Nelly gloomily. "I do not mind giving lemonade, but I really cannot learn to live in a bathtub."

"No indeed, and at any other time, I would not ask you to, Nelly," said Mrs. Pepin. "But it is a bit of a rush we're in right now. I'm sure you understand. Dinner guests. What a nuisance, but there you are."

"Are you suggesting I STAY in this tub?" roared Nelly. There are limits to even a cow's patience.

"Well, just for a bit. Approximately how long? Hmm." Mrs. Pepin pondered. "The guests come at three. Before-dinner chitchat, not to seem too greedy to get to the chow, taking maybe, oh, twenty, thirty minutes tops. Toddle over to the table, sit down, pass around the food, another ten minutes. Eat, eat, eat, let's say an hour. Push chairs back, don't look too anxious to arise from table, not there just for food, another fifteen, maybe twenty-five minutes, depending on how genteel they wish to appear. Mr. Bradshaw usually good for four minutes thirty-seven seconds, but this Miss Howndogger, still a dark horse, give her possibly another twenty minutes. Various napkin droppings, insincere offers of help in the kitchen, settle in living room, possibly on porch—weather permitting—sip some coffee, offer some more, Miss Howndogger doesn't wish to appear not to like hosts' coffee, so allow for several cups, another half hour. Finally toddle on home, which brings us to five twenty-five before we can again try to get you out of the tub, Nelly. Hope you don't mind."

"Hope I don't *MIND*?" said Nelly, spluttering. "Just what am I supposed to do here until then?"

"Why don't you . . . ? Hmmm. Why don't you . . . ?" faltered Mrs. Pepin. "I know, Nelly, why don't you take a bath? Here, have some bubbles." Mrs. Pepin handed Nelly her good gardenia bub-

THE PEPINS BEHAVE LIKE RELICS

ble bath and pushed everyone out of the bathroom. "There, that's that. Now hurry, we must
hunt up six place settings, and we can worry about
finding the rest another day."

The Pepins hunted for an hour and a half.
They looked under chairs, behind pictures, in closets, in vases, drawers, and canisters. They checked
drainpipes, shoes, rafters and eaves, the attic, the
basement, and the family room. They found only
one spoon, and it didn't even appear to belong to
them. A rogue spoon.

"Where can we have been eating?" moaned
Mrs. Pepin, wringing her hands. "And what are we
to do? We can't tell our guests to eat with their
hands."

"Yes you can," said Mr. Pepin, coming in wearing a sheet over his head.

"Mr. Pepin, please do not take to wearing the
linens. This is no time to pretend you are a futon,"
said Mrs. Pepin wearily.

"Visual aid, my dear," said Mr. Pepin, kissing
her merrily on the cheek. "Because I know exactly
what we are to do. If we cannot eat with forks and
knives, we must indeed eat with our hands."

"NO!" cried Mrs. Pepin. "I promised my Great-aunt Hildegarde at the wedding that our marriage would not come to this."

"Ah," said Mr. Pepin. "And indeed, your great-aunt had the right idea. We must live genteelly, but she had forgotten the Bedouins!"

"She so often did forget the Bedouins!" said Mrs. Pepin.

"Ah yes, the Bedouins!" said Roy and Miranda, who had read of such things.

"A few cushions on the floor," said Petunia.

"A small sandstorm," said Irving.

"Perhaps a camel or two," called Nelly from the bathroom, where she was recovering her good humor amongst the bubbles.

"But I have no Bedouin recipes!" said Mrs. Pepin, nervously running to her recipe file.

"Quick, to the library for Bedouin cookbooks," said Irving.

"And from there to the grocery store," said Petunia.

"We have no time to go hither and thither," said Mrs. Pepin. "We have time for either hither or thither but not both."

"Why don't you split up and use Irving's high-powered special radiophones?" called Nelly, who was discovering that, like many of us, she got her best ideas in the bath.

"Of course!" said Irving. "I will go to the library, I will radiophone to Petunia at the grocery store to let her know what Mother needs to make the Bedouin meal, while at home Mother decorates the floor with cushions, and Father goes to Bumblebee's Miserable Pet Shop for a camel."

"What are we," asked Roy, referring to himself and Miranda, "chopped liver?"

"No, you are lookouts," said Irving, patting him kindly. "You must sit on the roof and let us know when the guests approach."

"Nobody asked for my solution," said Roy to Miranda as they climbed up the drainpipe.

"Did you have a solution?" said Miranda.

"Of course. Why didn't they just put dinner in a dog bowl on the floor and get down on all fours and see how the other half lives? They might try some kibble while they're at it and see how it compares to, say, a nice vintage meat loaf."

"Do not be sour," said Miranda. "It will only

give you wrinkles and make you look like a basset hound."

"I'm just amazed they never came up with that one themselves. Not," grumbled Roy. They waited ten minutes on the roof, and then Roy got bored and built them another larger lightweight aircraft, and this time they sailed all the way to Forks of Cacapon.

In the meantime, Irving's plan worked like a charm. He found all the necessary ingredients for a splendid Bedouin meal, which he radiophoned to Petunia, who bought the groceries and flat bread and ran them home to Mrs. Pepin, who whipped up a Bedouin meal in a trice. The camel was somewhat less of a triumph because they were not able to fit it through the front door, and it immediately alerted their guests to what they had hoped would be a surprise.

"Ah, a camel. Are we having a Bedouin meal?" asked Mr. Bradshaw as he approached the Pepins' house with his *amour* at his side.

"Goody," said Miss Howndogger. "I love to eat with my hands."

It was a splendid repast. Mrs. Pepin had roasted several things inside of each other and then forgotten what was in what, so that a guessing game arose naturally as the meal progressed. After dinner, when the guests were about to depart, forty minutes ahead of schedule, because Miss Howndogger was less intimidated than Mrs. Pepin thought appropriate, Miss Howndogger looked upward and said, "Is there a cow in your bathtub?"

"How did you guess?" asked Mrs. Pepin.

"I'm funny that way," said Miss Howndogger, and it was then that the Pepins knew that Miss Howndogger would fit right in.

Afterward, when the lovebirds had gone off for an evening stroll and the Pepins were lazing about the porch, having finally hired a crane to haul Nelly out of the tub, so that she was eating peacefully once more in the barn, and they had opened the telegram from Roy saying he and Miranda would be making their way back from Forks of Cacapon any time now, Mr. Pepin said to Mrs. Pepin, "My dear, not only have we solved our problems

ourselves this fine day but we did so as a family. Each playing his or her part in a solution."

"My heavens," said Mrs. Pepin, thinking back, "you are right. Mr. Pepin used flags and Morse code to alert Mr. Bradshaw that he must invent a way to get Nelly onto the roof. Petunia found the fork in Nelly's hoof. I suggested a hunt for the cutlery. Mr. Pepin suggested a Bedouin dinner. Nelly thought of the radiophones, and Irving assigned us each a task. And we all decided to hire the crane to get Nelly out of the bathtub."

"But if we solve our problems ourselves, what will the readers do?" asked Petunia.

"You cannot suggest, dear Mother and Father, that they simply read?" implored Irving.

"Not when they are so used to taking part," said Petunia.

"Not at all, not at all," said Mr. Pepin. "But we Pepins have clearly learned from our readers. Solutions begin to spring to mind where once there were only dust motes. And because of that, and because lately we have been spending all our time at gymnastics and bowling and town council and soccer and—"

"Yes?" said Mrs. Pepin. If they listed all their activities, they would never get off the porch.

"Well, my dear, with summer vacation here, I propose some true Pepin time. Let us forget all these activities we have attempted to cram into our summer and instead jam all of us, Roy, Miranda, and Nelly, too, into our automobile and sally forth."

"Oh yes," breathed Mrs. Pepin excitedly, "let us sally."

"A family vacation!" said Irving, ever swift on the uptake.

"A road trip!" said Petunia.

"But to where?" asked Mrs. Pepin.

"Why, to Tinton Falls, New Jersey; Lake Nebagamon, Wisconsin; Normal, Illinois; Wiggonsville, Ohio; Pottsville, Pennsylvania; Vinton, Iowa; Miami, Oklahoma; Kalamazoo, Michigan; Grow, Texas; North Livermore, Maine; Miami, Missouri; Walkerton, Indiana; Mendota Heights, Minnesota; Hughes, Alaska; Good Hope, Georgia; Yazoo City, Mississippi; Nanafalia, Alabama; Skullbone, Tennessee; Low Moor, Virginia; Mesita, New Mexico; Boring, Maryland; Bohemia, Louisiana; Croton-on-Hudson, New York; Delight, Arkansas; Lone Elm, Kansas; Smoke Signal, Arizona; Zigzag, Oregon; East and West Braintree, Vermont; Reepsville, North Carolina; Brookline, Massachusetts; Hanover, New Hampshire; Peanut, California; Stamping Ground, Kentucky; Shaft Ox Corner, Delaware; Plentywood, Montana; Funk, Nebraska; Rainbow and Hazardville, Connecticut; Bonetrail,

North Dakota; Ideal, South Dakota; Ten Sleep, Wyoming; Two Egg, Florida; New Harmony, Utah; Last Chance, Colorado; Captain Cook, Hawaii; Sedro-Woolley, Washington; Washington, D.C.; Duckwater, Nevada; Atomic City, Idaho; Coosawhatchie, South Carolina; Great Swamp, Worden Pond, and Yawgoo Pond, Rhode Island; Ikes Fork, Slaty Fork, Northfork, Sand Fork, Glen Fork, Forks of Cacapon, Lost River, Lost Creek, and Lost City, West Virginia; and Mashpee, Massachusetts, to thank all our dear readers personally for their solutions," said Mr. Pepin.

"To the Pepinmobile!" said Mrs. Pepin, scooping up Roy and Miranda, who had just arrived home.

"To the Pepinmobile!" they all sang, climbing into the car and heading into the vast grandeur of the American open road.

"Are we there yet?" asked Nelly.

GOFISH

POLLY HORVATH

What did you want to be when you grew up?
I wanted to be a writer, a dancer, and a nun.

What was your worst subject in school?
Math. When I got to geometry in tenth grade, it made me weep.

Where do you write your books?
I have an office in our basement. It's very private with a window overlooking a lot of fruit trees where the horse likes to graze. He snorts, I write. Sometimes, I snort. I don't know if he writes.

Which of your characters is most like you?
Uncle Martin in *The Corps of the Bare-Boned Plane*.

Are you a morning person or a night owl?
I'm a morning person. When I'm doing a first draft, I have to work in the morning.

What's your idea of the best meal ever?
Cheese and crackers, and red wine. Or lobster and clams at a lobster pound in Maine. Or a cruiser day lunch, which only people who have gone to Camp Nebagamon will understand.

Which do you like better: cats or dogs?
Dogs. I love dogs. I could never live without a dog.

What do you value most in your friends?
Tolerance and finding the same things funny that I do.

Where do you go for peace and quiet?
We live in miles of wilderness on our doorstep, so generally, I just go outdoors.

What's your favorite song?
"Hallelujah" by Leonard Cohen, sung by Rufus Wainwright.

Who is your favorite fictional character?
Jo March or anyone from *Sweet Thursday* by John Steinbeck, which is my favorite book.

What are you most afraid of?
Something happening to the people I love.

What time of the year do you like best?
Autumn, around Halloween, when everything is golden.

If you were stranded on a desert island, who would you want for company?
My husband, daughters, our dog, and our horse. Then, I wouldn't be stranded.

*K*eep reading for an excerpt from
Polly Horvath's **Everything on a Waffle**,
coming soon in paperback from Square Fish Books.

EXCERPT

I live in Coal Harbour, British Columbia. I have never lived anyplace else. My name is Primrose Squarp. I am eleven years old. I have hair the color of carrots in an apricot glaze (recipe to follow), skin fair and clear where it isn't freckled, and eyes like summer storms.

One June day a typhoon arose at sea that blew the rain practically perpendicular to our house. My father's fishing boat was late getting in and my mother, who wasn't one for sitting around biting her nails, put on her yellow macintosh and hat and took me over to Miss Perfidy's house, saying, "Miss Perfidy, John is out there somewhere and I don't know if his boat is coming safely into shore, so I am going out in our sailboat to find him." Well, a thinking person might have told my mother that if a big fishing boat wasn't going to make it through those waves, our little skiff sure wasn't. But Miss Perfidy wasn't one to waste time in idle chitchat. She just nodded. And that was the last I saw of my mother.

The fishing boat never came back to shore. Neither did the skiff. So all that June I continued to live with Miss Perfidy. There was a memorial service for my parents but I wouldn't go. I knew that my parents hadn't drowned. I suspected that they had washed up on an island somewhere and were waiting to be rescued. Every morning I went down to the docks to watch the boats come in, sure that I would see my parents towed in, perhaps on the back of a whale.

"I don't know what you think the story of Jonah is about, Miss Perfidy," I said. "But to me it is about how hopeful the human heart is. I am certain my parents, if not in the belly of a whale, are wondering how I am doing and trying to get home to me!" I called the last few words out in the direction Miss Perfidy had gone. She often stalked off when I was in the middle of a sentence. It didn't encourage many heartfelt confidences.

I didn't mind Miss Perfidy's exits, but what I did mind was her mothball smell, which was never overwhelming yet hovered around her in a little fog. Mothballs spilled from every drawer in her house. I couldn't understand why Miss Perfidy seemed to be the only person in town who had such a huge problem with moths. One day I got out a box and read the directions. "You know, Miss Perfidy," I said, "is it possible that you misunderstood the directions? You seem to be using an awful lot of mothballs." But Miss Perfidy had already left the room.

Besides, it wasn't really any of my business. The town council was paying Miss Perfidy her usual baby-sitting fee of three dollars an hour from what they called the Squarps' estate and what I called my parents' bank account until they could figure out what to do with me. This was taking them a lot longer than it might have because my parents hadn't made wills or thought ahead to the day when they would both disappear at sea. But even I knew that at three dollars an hour I wasn't long for life with Miss Perfidy.

One member of the town council argued that three dollars an hour was a lot to pay a baby-sitter for those endless night hours when I was asleep and Miss Perfidy was snoring in her own bed, but it was fruitless to argue with Miss Perfidy. She was mean with money. In Coal Harbour there was whaling and fishing and the navy. If you didn't whale or fish or do naval things you had to do what you could to hold body and soul together, so Miss Perfidy was tight with her pennies by necessity. When things had gotten too tight a few years back she had sold her small cottage and bought an even smaller cottage. Before she moved from the small cottage she dug up her flower bulbs one by one—tulips, daffodils, crocuses—and not being a real stinker, neatly filled in all the holes again. When the realtor heard about it, he came charging over. "Miss Perfidy," he had said. "You just can't do this. People expect you to leave your flowers." But she said she had paid for and planted every last bulb and she was taking every last bulb, and speaking of bulbs she was also unscrewing and taking all the lightbulbs. Land's sakes, did he want her to leave her clothes for the new owners too?

Toward the beginning of August, when the town council finally decided to invite me to a meeting to discuss my fate, they sent Miss Honeycut, the school guidance counselor, to escort me and Miss Perfidy. Miss Honeycut was the closest thing Coal Harbour had to a psychiatrist, which wasn't really very close at all. Everyone knew that Miss Honeycut was born to the British aristocracy and was going to inherit half of Yorkshire, England, when her father, still kicking around at eighty-three, died. People were very, very nice to her because they thought that maybe someday she would remember them in her will. Or at least invite them to visit her manor house in Yorkshire when she finally got her mitts on it. Only my mother had avoided Miss Honeycut. She said that despite Miss Honeycut's vast global experience, she was a bore. That she talked exclusively in anecdotes and couldn't converse like normal people and that the reason she was stuck way across the world in Coal Harbour was that it was the only place she could get a job and that because her father knew the principal of Coal Harbour Elementary.

But I wished I could hear more about the places Miss Honeycut had traveled and the things she had seen. I remember her telling my mother that as a little girl she had learned to play bridge riding a train through China. It didn't seem fair that when she was my age she had already learned more about the world than perhaps I would ever have the chance to.

When Miss Honeycut came to the door, Miss Perfidy and I were ready. Miss Perfidy was wearing a very old tweed suit and carrying a black patent leather handbag over her forearm. Miss Perfidy knew that no one would want to tussle with someone in such a Queen of England getup and that this gave her the upper hand. She was never happy unless she had the upper hand. Unfortunately, neither was Miss Honeycut and she looked at Miss Perfidy as if a tuna fish had just died on her foot.

All the way to the meeting Miss Honeycut kept saying how sorry she was that my parents had died, and she said "died" in a very pointed way until I finally explained that she must be mistaken and I was content to wait for my parents' return no matter how long it took. Miss Honeycut said that this was a most unrealistic attitude and that I must think of my future. Miss Perfidy didn't say anything the whole way there but sniffed disapprovingly at both of us.

In the meeting hall we took seats near the front, waiting for more people to drift in. Miss Perfidy continued to sniff. She sniffed so heartily people in rows forward and back of her began sniffing to detect what Miss Perfidy smelled. Soon nearly everyone was sniffing.

"They've all got colds," grumbled Miss Perfidy, turning to look accusingly at me. "Big crowd packed into a small hall. We're all going to get sick now."

I didn't know what to say, so I looked at my feet, then got out my mother's memo pad, which I kept in my back pocket. It had fallen out of my mother's raincoat when she left me at Miss Perfidy's. There wasn't much in there, just her recipe for carrots in an apricot glaze and an old grocery list. The rest of the pages were blank. I read and reread the recipe as we sat waiting for the meeting to start.

When the last person had drifted in and had a sniff, Miss Honeycut started the meeting by saying that my parents' bank account was dwindling and, as imperfect an arrangement as she thought it might be to have me move in with a relative I didn't even know, the town council must try to summon my next of kin, Mr. Jack Dion, because, after all this time, he was the only kin they could find any reference to and no one else was volunteering to take me in.

Well, good luck to you, I thought because the one time my mother had mentioned Uncle Jack, her brother, to me, she had said he was a drifter. "Old hotfoot Jack" she called him. Miss Honeycut had found out that he was in the navy now, stationed all the way across the country in Halifax, Nova Scotia.

I figured it would be a miracle if he ended up in Coal Harbour, but that's exactly what did happen. After the meeting, the council contacted Uncle Jack at sea and he said he couldn't come, but immediately after that, the navy shifted everyone around and he got shifted right onto the base in Coal Harbour, which the town council thought was very fortuitous as he could take care of this mess, by which they meant me.

As soon as Uncle Jack arrived, he was whisked off to a town council meeting. When Uncle Jack, who was tall, mustached, broad-shouldered, blond, and ruddy, walked into the room, Miss Honeycut eyed him thoughtfully. This surprised me because Uncle Jack looked like a pig, albeit a lean, good-looking pig, whereas Miss Honeycut looked more like a turtle. It was hard to imagine a pig and a turtle together but it gave me something to do through the rest of the meeting.

The council reminded Uncle Jack that I was still hanging out at Miss Perfidy's waiting to be claimed and costing three dollars an hour. Uncle Jack seemed confused when they told him this. He had assumed that when he said no, the town council had found some other relative or guardian for me. He explained that he was a training officer and had just moved into a small house connected to the gym on the base. It was very convenient for him because he taught classes in the gym and worked out there every day but he wouldn't be allowed to keep a child there. If he wanted to do that, he would have to move to the family housing part of the base. And he really didn't want to do that. The town council looked horrified when he told them this. They had wanted him to go all gooey when he saw me. I didn't. I admired his honesty. After all, we both had lives already in gear.

The meeting dragged on and on because as usual there were three people who loved to hear themselves talk and wouldn't shut up and it took the moderator a long time to figure out that none of them had anything to say. They exhausted everyone so much that the most that could be decided was that Uncle Jack should think about things, and they left it at that. Everyone broke for cake and coffee.

Miss Honeycut noodled her way up to Uncle Jack with an extra piece of cake. What he was supposed to do with it I didn't know because he already had a piece on his plate and another jammed up his cheek. Since I had finished my piece, I said I'd take it. Miss Honeycut gave me a look. She handed me the cake, though, since Uncle Jack was watching. Then Miss Honeycut started telling Uncle Jack that she never thought he should have been asked to take a child on. How she felt it was an awful imposition for a bachelor, relative or no, ho ho ho. How he needn't feel badly about not being up to the challenge. Uncle Jack looked at her coolly when she said this. Miss Honeycut went on swiftly—an officer's job was challenging enough. She knew. Her father had been an officer. It was such a startling about-face position that I stood with my mouth hanging slightly open, full of half-eaten cake. Miss Honeycut went on to say how there were many excellent foster homes for children like me and people did, despite what you heard, frequently adopt the older child, and that's when Uncle Jack put his arm around me and said he had decided to take care of me himself. It was a nice warm hug and the first real human contact I had had since this whole business began. And it was comforting, even though I knew he had only done it to spite Miss Honeycut.

"Don't worry," I said to Uncle Jack later on, "I don't expect it will be for long. I'm sure my mother and father will be here anytime now."

Then the navy sent its Coal Harbour troops on a peacekeeping mission and announced the government's decision to close down the base permanently. The town thought Uncle Jack was going too and they were back to square one. That's when he surprised everyone by quitting the navy, getting into real estate, and buying the house connected to the gym on the base. It was, he said, a good deal because he got the gym thrown in for free. He really loved that gym.

And so I ended up with my clothes and things in three houses: the house that Uncle Jack bought, Miss Perfidy's house, where I continued to keep the sweaters that my mom had knit for me so they would be moth-free, and my own house, which Uncle Jack put up for rent. It sent me deeper into a funny, detached, dreamlike state. I do not live anywhere anymore, I said to myself on one of my walks down to the pier to wait for my parents. I am not in the body of life. I hover on the extremities. I float.

Carrots in an Apricot Glaze

Take a package of carrots and scrape them. Chop the carrots into bite-sized pieces. Open a tin of apricots. Save them for something else and pour the juice into the pan with the carrots and a little water. Add 2 tablespoons of butter and 3 tablespoons of brown sugar—more if you like them sweeter, less if you don't. Boil them until the carrots are tender, adding water if the liquid starts to disappear and a glaze appears before the carrots are cooked. The liquid should boil down and turn into a glaze just as the carrots become tender.